VIGILANTE

A GIA SANTELLA CRIME THRILLER
BOOK 2

KRISTI BELCAMINO

LIQUID MIND PUBLISHING

Liquid Mind Publishing
This is a work of fiction. All characters, names, places and events are the product of the author's imagination or used fictitiously.

To my readers — none of this would be possible without you and your support! Grazie mille!

GIA SANTELLA CRIME THRILLER SERIES

Enjoying the Gia Santella series? Scan below to order more books today!

Vendetta

Vigilante

Vengeance

Black Widow

Day of the Dead

Border Line

Night Fall

Stone Cold

Cold as Death

Cold Blooded

Dark Shadows

Dark Vengeance

Dark Justice

Deadly Justice

Deadly Lies

PROLOGUE

THE GRAVEYARD WAS MY SANCTUARY.

With nearly everyone I loved dead, it was the one place I felt at home. The only place I truly felt comfortable in my skin.

Today, I was visiting my friend Ethel Swanson's grave. I made the trip across the Bay to the Berkeley cemetery every few weeks so I wouldn't forget that she had died because of me. I had vowed—well, made a promise at her grave—that I would make sure she was never forgotten.

My favorite time to visit Ethel was at sunset, when the dipping sun made the Golden Gate bridge glow and turned the waves of the bay into sparkling silvery shimmers of light.

Yesterday, I'd driven to Monterey to put flowers on my family's graves. Pink roses for my mother. Sunflowers for my father. Nothing for my brother. I often found others had left flowers on my parents' plots. My brother's grave remained barren. His was closer to the fence and set apart from the other family plots. The grass around it was less green, more overgrown with weeds, as if even the caretakers were wont to neglect his final resting place.

His murder was still unsolved. And I didn't care.

The man who killed my parents had died at my hands. That was all that mattered.

After a cursory glance at Christopher's grave, I'd crossed my legs and sat on the grass to talk to my mother and father about my life. It was pretty much the same script every month: I told them that I was a failure, that I had moments of clarity when I stopped drinking and doing drugs, and sleeping around, but that I was still a hot mess. I told them about Bobby and our long-distance relationship. About how he seemed wonderful and how that scared the hell out of me.

Of course, I never shared like that with Ethel.

Today, I stood at her gravestone and rearranged the red roses I had delivered there every week. Once upon a time, Ethel had confessed to me how she ended up on the streets. Her jerk husband used to beat her nearly to death and then in typical abuser-fashion would beg her forgiveness by offering red roses and empty promises.

The only thing that stopped his abuse was a knife to the heart one night when he was sleeping. Years later, when Ethel was released from prison, she couldn't find work and turned to drinking. Soon, she ended up on the streets begging.

We'd become pals when I moved into the Tenderloin neighborhood and she camped outside my building.

And then, a few months ago, she'd ended up dead. Strangled with a playing card, the one-eyed jack, stuffed down her throat.

The Tenderloin newspaper ran a brief obituary.

ETHEL SWANSON had dreamed of being an actress ever since she was a little girl. She certainly had the personality and name for it. However, when she fell in love with the wrong man, her dreams were shattered, said friend Gia Santella. She never quite recovered from her abusive marriage and ended up on the streets of the Tenderloin where she was beloved by all. She died violently, but she will never be forgotten. She is buried underneath a flowering tree in the Oakland hills and has red roses delivered to her grave every week. "Because she mattered," Santella said. Ethel Swanson was 70.

As the sun set and the stars rose above, I traced my fingers over Ethel's gravestone.

"I'm sorry, Miss Ethel. I'm so goddamn sorry you're there and I'm here. It's all my fault. I wish I could make it up to you."

1

ITALIAN STALLION

THE NEXT MORNING, DANTE SIDE-EYED ME AS I STEPPED OUT OF THE elevator into the penthouse lobby of my father's company. Instead of his usual brilliant white smile, Dante frowned.

"What?" I asked, scowling. I was in a bad mood. Getting up at the freaking crack of dawn—okay before noon—did not suit me. The fog hadn't even lifted from my San Francisco neighborhood yet.

And meeting with stuffy board members was high on my list of things I never wanted to do in my lifetime.

But now that my father, brother, and godfather were dead, I'd been left in charge. For whatever reason, I was now the CEO. Something I had never wanted and still didn't.

The penthouse lobby looked nothing like it had when my dad was alive. It now had plush red carpet and was scattered with black onyx pedestals holding oddly familiar-shaped obelisks nearly as big as me. Two walls were covered in mirrors. I drew my gaze back to my agitated friend. While his silky black hair swept back from his face like the Italian Stallion he was, his olive skin was slightly ashen.

"What's wrong? Are you feeling okay? You look a little pale." I reached over and felt his forehead. "Yeah, you're a little clammy."

Dante let out an exasperated sigh and as always, perfectly enunciated his words. "*That* is what you are wearing?"

Spoken like a ridiculously stylish gay man. I gaped at him. Then realized he was serious.

"Sure." I knew I sounded defensive. "Why not?"

I tried not to notice the contrast between my outfit and his exquisite, custom-fit Italian suit.

Dante waited to speak until a woman in an old-fashioned black-and-white maid uniform finished dusting the obnoxious white marble sculpture near us.

"You're going to introduce yourself to the board wearing black leather pants?"

"At least I wore my nicest pair." I was starting to get angry.

He closed his eyes, clearly frustrated beyond words.

I took another look at Dante, a little worried. He *had* felt clammy. And now his face was contorted. His mouth opened and closed and his nostrils flared. Was he doing deep breathing? Counting to ten?

"And that ... that shirt," he finally said, opening his eyes. "You know they can fire you."

Good, I thought, but bit my tongue.

"Fine. I'll put on my jacket." I shrugged on my black blazer. It partially concealed my white T-shirt that said "Fuck Authority" below a picture of a skull and crossbones.

The woman was now dusting an enormous white phallic symbol right beside me.

Dante looked pained. "What about the three Armani suits I bought for you last week?"

Is that what all this was about? I'd pay him back. But I knew it wasn't that. His feelings were hurt. His unerring sense of style was offended.

I shrugged. "They're cute." *If you want to look like you have a stick up your ass.*

He made a jerking motion to pop his wrist out of his sleeve. He looked at his TAG Heuer and then glanced over at the door leading to the boardroom.

"What now? Are we late, too?" I rolled my eyes and leaned back against the mirrored wall.

He met my eyes. "We might have time for you to change. I can run you back to your place. We can be a few minutes late."

I smiled, pushed away from the wall and headed toward the boardroom door.

He winced. He knew he'd lost.

"What you don't seem to get," I said over my shoulder, "is that I don't care what they think. I don't want to be here. I don't want anything to do with running this company or the stuffy old men on the board." I knew I sounded like a pouty five-year-old and I didn't care. It seemed like the woman in the maid outfit was looking for something to do closer to us. Eavesdropping. Fine by me. I didn't care who knew what I thought.

Dante caught up to me. "Gia! You've never met any of them."

"They all stood by and let my godfather drive my father's business into the ground. They never said a word. They never reached out to me even once. And now that I'm in charge, I'm only sticking around long enough to replace every goddamn one of them."

The woman audibly gasped. We both swiveled our heads toward her and she clamped her hand over her mouth.

"Excuse me," I said, gesturing with one finger. "Come over here for a second."

Her cheeks grew red.

I stuck out my hand. "I'm Gia. What's your name?"

"Carmen."

"Nice to meet you, Carmen. I got to ask you something," I said. "Do you like wearing that outfit? Tell me the truth? I promise your job won't be affected."

"No." Her voice was quiet.

"I'm sorry I couldn't hear you."

"No, I don't like it."

"I didn't think you did. It's like *Gone with the Wind* or something."

She smiled, but still looked nervous.

"Do you like your job here?"

"*Si.* I mean yes." She nodded fervently.

"I mean, would you rather work here or say at some apartment building in Russian Hill?" *Like my building.* "I could find you a job where you have less work and more money and don't have to wear a stupid get up like that."

"I like it here, really. The uniform, no? But I like working here." She shrugged. "I do what I want. Nobody bothers me. Make my own hours."

I bit my lip thinking about. "You're being honest, right?"

"Yes."

"Okay. But the uniform has to go." I squinted at her. "What are the stuffed shirts paying you?"

She named some absurdly pithy amount. "I'll double that right now. And you can wear whatever the hell you want to work every day. If anyone says anything, tell them Gia Santella told you herself."

"Okay." She gave a small smile and slipped out a nearby door.

Dante touched my elbow. "Back to what we were talking about. You can't fire them. They are elected by the stockholders. What if there are some good men on the board?"

"If I have to be the CEO—which apparently is what my father wanted—then I'll damn well do whatever it takes to root out the rotten ones and make sure they get kicked off the board. Plus, your job is to help me do that."

"What?" his eyes grew wide. I'd asked him to be my advisor, but had never elaborated on his job duties.

"You're nice. You're nonjudgmental. If anyone can determine who is worth keeping around and who isn't, it's you. Together, we can weed out the toxic ones."

"Gia! I don't want that responsibility. Good grief."

He was so cute when he swore.

"I need your help." This time my voice was quiet. It was true. I needed Dante. I didn't want to face these men on my own.

Dante ran a hand through his hair and sighed, nodding. He was in.

But then he touched my elbow again and made a face. "Leather pants?"

"Yup." I gave him another smile. "With these pants and a senator's husband at my side, they wouldn't dare fuck with me."

"We are not married yet."

"Speaking of that, are you sure you want to get married this young? I mean, I adore Matt, but, dude, you're just a baby."

"I'm nearly twenty-five."

I put my finger on my chin. "Which means you're twenty-four."

But his twenty-four was probably like my forty. I didn't want to admit it, but Dante had acted like a mature, responsible, adult since we were twelve-years-old. The opposite of me.

"Back to your outfit," he said, raising an eyebrow.

"I'd rather talk about you." I gave him my sweetest smile. Which he ignored.

"What about the Armani? You realize they cost me a small fortune, Gia."

Now, he was just griping. He thought nothing of dropping several grand on an outfit. In that way, we were alike.

"Like I said, they're cute. I'll wear the black one to the next board meeting."

"You will?"

He sounded so damn happy.

"Sure."

I sighed. After all these years, he still believed my lies.

2

BLOOD MONEY

INHALING SHARPLY, I TUGGED ON THE HEAVY OAK DOOR TO THE BOARD room. Before I stepped inside, I breathed out slowly. My stomach was a bundle of live wires. I'd put on a good show of bravado for Dante, but the truth was I was scared as hell. Words I'd learned studying karate came back to me.

The ability to quiet one's mind is essential to center a warrior's greatest power and strength. Dominance is not overpowering or showy, but lies in those who carry it inside. The true warrior will send ripples of influence into every space they enter.

I needed some of those ripples right now. I stepped inside the room. At first, the light from the floor-to-ceiling windows was blinding. As my eyes adjusted, the sweeping views of the Golden Gate Bridge and Pacific Ocean far below made me dizzy.

The board room was more austere than its pimped-out lobby. The space was as sterile and sanitized as an operating room and made me want to whisper.

When we walked in we were greeted by ten frowns from ten uptight assholes in—what else? —Armani suits. They all blended into one. Gray hair, red ties, pinched expressions. Snobbery and disdain dripped from their signet rings.

Dante tensed beside me. These old-school dudes were not friendly to gay men, I could tell. I felt like telling them, "Be nice to my best friend because your future is in his hands. One word from him and it's sayonara, baby."

The big cushy leather chair at the head of the table was vacant, waiting for me. I thought that was a good sign. I'd fully expected some Thurston Howell the Third type to be manspreading in the seat. Unfortunately, the empty spot was at the far side of the room, in front of the massive bank of windows. A long walk from where I stood.

Pulling my shoulders back, I struck out for the chair, which suddenly seemed miles away. It was as if the air was sucked out of the room as I walked. I swallowed and the noise of my gulp seemed to echo. When I neared the chair, I grabbed one of the chairs lining the wall and pulled it up beside my big plush leather one.

I gestured for Dante to sit by me. He was literally my right-hand man, now.

The goddamn leather chair was on its lowest level. I could practically rest my forehead on the gleaming wood table before me. It made me feel small and insignificant. I caught one blue-haired old dude smirking. I reached down and fiddled with the chair adjustment for a few seconds but nothing happened. I still had table up to my armpits. Everyone stared. I cast a frantic glance at Dante, but he was busying shuffling papers. Finally, when one guy cleared his throat and the meeting began, I gave up. I sat as erect as I could so I didn't feel like a little kid at the adult table.

After I was introduced and gave a closed mouth smile, I sat back and listened to one old codger drone on about profit and loss yada yada blah blah. I was starting to fade. Dante nudged me. They'd asked me something.

"Oh, yeah, right."

I had no idea what I had agreed to. I was concentrating too hard on stifling my yawns and sitting up straight.

Dante frowned.

I opened my eyes wide, blinking, and did a few jaw exercises. *Focus, Santella.*

As I tuned in to the droning voices I recognized some words and shot a look at Dante. Bloody hell. They were talking about the proposal I'd emailed this morning. Then one grumpy guy stood and cleared his throat. "Mr. Chairman. In my opinion, this proposal is not in the purview of the board. We don't approve or reject individual projects, such as the one Miss Santella has proposed. That is not our role. With that said, I move to reject as it is not something that seems to be in line with the objectives and goals of this company."

Dante gave me a sharp elbow to my ribs.

I jumped. I was on.

"Excuse me, gentlemen." I pushed back my chair and stood. It made me feel like an adult again.

"You are out of order!" I didn't hear who said it and I didn't care.

I had thought hard about what to say. After my parents' deaths, when my godfather ran the company, he developed a mixed-use facility in the Sunset called Bay View. The whole project was paid for with blood money. Before my godfather died, he drove a dying woman out of her home and probably took part in some other nefarious deeds to clear the way for the development. I later learned that when my father was alive, he'd tried to stop the project.

Now that they were both dead, I was in charge. My initial instinct had been to raze the whole damn thing, but the building was now almost finished. When my attorney, Sal, told me I was now CEO and had to make a decision on the development, I'd stayed awake nights for weeks trying to figure out what to do with it.

Then, after a bit too much tequila, the boy I was dating, Bobby, showed up at my door with a dozen roses. At three in the morning. He'd driven all the way from his home in Santa Cruz because he missed me, he said.

I saw the roses and burst into tears, which, of course, utterly confused him, as it should have.

It reminded me of Ethel, I said. Bobby listened as I explained.

When I was done, he did things to me that made me forget all about Ethel for quite a few hours.

But that's when I decided, in honor of Ethel, I was turning Bay View into housing for the homeless. A special innovative development that would not only house the residents but also employ them. The Tenderloin had no shortage of programs to help house the homeless, such as housing them in SROs—single resident occupancies, but I wanted to take it one step further.

In my development, the upper floors would be adorable studio apartments with galley kitchens and the street level businesses would remain the same as my godfather had planned: a restaurant, hair salon, flower shop, and a market with fresh fruit and vegetables. The rooftop would contain a full garden with fruit and vegetables that were used in the restaurant and sold in the market. However, in my plan, the residents had first dibs on jobs in the building.

Of course, I thought it was the greatest idea ever.

Apparently, the board thought differently.

Luckily, I didn't give a rat's ass what they thought.

Still standing, I placed my palms on the desk. "I'm sorry that you disagree with my proposal gentlemen, but as the CEO, I'm going to have to say ..." I looked at Dante. "Well, too bad."

Hey, it was a step up from what I wanted to say, which was "Sorry, Charlie."

One man couldn't contain himself. He'd been spluttering with rage since I spoke.

"But ... but ... the views. The views alone are million-dollar views."

"I know!" I said excitedly. "Isn't that great?"

"But they are homeless," one man spit the word out as if it were the most distasteful word he'd ever said.

"And?" I raised an eyebrow. Nobody spoke a word. "I guess what I'm hearing is that you don't think that homeless people appreciate a good view same as the rest of us?"

Silence.

"Would you go so far as to say that only rich, white old dudes like you can appreciate a great view?"

Not a peep.

"What about, let's say ... gay people? Do they appreciate a great view? How about black people? Native Americans? Mexicans?" I snapped my fingers. "I know ... how about Italian-Americans? Do you think they appreciate a view the same as you?"

Looking at all their faces, I could tell that each and every one of them wanted to punch me in the face. That was okay because I wanted to kick them in the family jewels.

"This meeting is adjourned." I pushed back my chair, stood and stalked toward the door.

At the door, I turned and said, "By the way, the name of the development is Swanson Place."

3

NO MERCY

SWEAT DRIPPED OFF MY TEMPLE, SPLASHING ONTO THE SMOOTH WOODEN floor of the dojo.

"Had enough?" Kato laughed, tightening the belt of his karategi.

"Hell, yes." I panted and wiped more sweat off my neck with a small white towel. "You mad at me or something?"

"Trying to prove my point." He watched me over the large water bottle he was guzzling.

I took a big sip of my water, eyeing him back. He looked like he'd just woken up from the most refreshing nap ever and was ready to tackle his day. He wasn't even breathing hard. Kato was in his forties and kept his sleek hair longer in the back. His eyes always sparkled with life, as if he were on the verge of telling you some marvelous secret about the world and its wonders.

But today those eyes saw right through me. And his words cut to the chase.

"Fine," I said with a huff. "I'll go on the wagon. Tomorrow."

"Today."

"Maybe."

A small part of me worried that even if I wanted to quit drinking for good I wouldn't be able to. It was how I'd dealt with my grief since my parents' deaths. I never said it was healthy. Or effective. It was what it was.

Other students starting pouring into the cavernous dojo for the next class. To the west, the setting sun cast a reddish glow on the city. The dojo was on the fourth floor of an old warehouse in Chinatown and had floor-to-ceiling windows in all but one direction. The wide-open space was calming, but it was the work I did there that kept me sane.

My new apartment would have a space for me to train, but I intended to keep coming to the dojo a few times a week. I needed Kato to motivate me. He had no mercy. My excuses were a joke to him. And rightly so.

He knew drugs and drinking made me weak. Not just physically, either. I stuffed my towel into my bag and turned to say goodbye. Kato was talking to a student, his forehead furrowed. He crooked a finger at me. I slipped over to listen.

"Are you sure?" Kato said to the young man.

"Haven't seen him for at least three days. You told me to let you know."

The student walked away.

I took another swig of my water and waited for Kato to speak.

"Wyatt—the homeless man who Matt sees on the way to work every day for the past fifteen years—is gone. That makes three."

"There's something going on."

"I agree," he said. His eyebrows scrunched together. "I don't like it," he said.

"Me, either."

A streak of dread ran down my back.

It was as if I could sense evil heading my way.

4

FOXY HEIGHTS

DARLING'S SHOP WAS IN THE HEART OF THE T.L. IT CATERED TO everyone from the absurdly rich women living on Nob Hill to the accountant slogging away in the financial district to the homeless woman begging for food on the street corner.

Because the Tenderloin took care of its own. On the first Tuesday of each month, the salon's stylists dedicated their time to give free services to the neighborhood's down and out. They could afford to be generous. Darling owned the busiest hair salon in San Francisco. It stretched for nearly a block and some thirty stylists worked there.

After showering, I headed over there to bitch about the board, get my butt kicked in cribbage, and catch up on the neighborhood gossip. I walked so I could bring my dog Django and check on construction of my new home. My old building in the Tenderloin had burned down. A crazy Italian man—who'd killed my parents and thought I was his daughter—had paid someone to torch it. He was dead now. The new building was going up in the same space, in an area known as the Panhandle because of its homeless population.

The Panhandle was surrounded by other T.L. neighborhoods, including the Forgotten Island, the Nipple, Pill Hill, the Whoa-Man,

Fecal Fountain, and Foxy Heights—where Darling's salon was located.

The salon was like an exotic land to me.

Tonight, the silver chairs in the salon were filled and half a dozen women waited their turn, lounging in pink velvet armchairs in the lobby. Laughter and small talk greeted me when I walked in. The smell of hair product and heady perfumes filled the air. High-heeled Jimmy Choo's peeked out from underneath black plastic smocks. Eyes and lips were made up to perfection. It was a typical Friday night at the salon: These women were getting their hair done and then heading out on the town, to sushi and theater and clubs with live music.

I was born missing the hair fixing gene, but worse than that, I was born missing the desire to have cute hair at all. My long dark hair was layered and sleek only because Dante had made me a standing appointment with his friend. Phillipe showed up at my apartment early every second Monday morning when I was sleeping and couldn't escape.

Although Darling's shop was lucrative, her main business took place in the back room. It was outfitted like a cozy living room in a mansion with a TV that took up one entire wall and a grouping of white leather couches. The back room was where her "other" business was conducted, the one that earned her enough money to buy her a house on Nob Hill *and* in the Oakland Hills. It involved the procurement of paperwork, the expensive and hard to get kind: fake IDs, passports, anything someone would want to disappear.

Sitting at a table in the back room, we did shots of Jack Daniels and played cribbage on a wooden board that was shaped like the state of Louisiana for some reason. We were one quarter of the way into the bottle and nearing the end of our first game.

"How's your place coming along, baby girl?" Darling asked, expertly dealing six cards, her long, gold-painted fingernails catching the light. The cards slid across the sleek table and piled up in a neat stack before me. Her lioness mane of dark curls bobbed as she dealt, along with her ample bosom.

"Still not fast enough for me," I said. "Maybe two more weeks?"

I scooped up my cards. Darling flipped the cut card and I froze. I had a twenty-four hand. Nearly the best hand you could get. I tried to plaster on my poker face. I was not lucky. I was far from lucky. And yet, there it was—a goddamn twenty-four hand. Three threes and a nine and the cut card was a three. Mother fucker.

I glanced at Darling from under my eyelashes and caught her watching me with her golden cat eyes, lined thickly with kohl like the Egyptian goddess she was probably re-incarnated from.

"Good. You need to get back to the hood. We miss you. Well, mainly miss seeing that mutt around." When we'd lived in the Tenderloin before, I'd tried to swing by the salon at least once a day with Django because he was crazy about Darling. And she was bonkers about him. Django, a pit bull-lab mix, was like a best friend, lie detector, and bodyguard rolled into one. He could spot trouble from a block away. If you were bad news, you'd trigger Django's low guttural growl and raise his hackles, even if you were a four-foot-eleven, ninety-pounder who seemed harmless. Hulking, muscled six-foot-tall men like Darling's bouncer, George, only garnered whole body wiggles and licks from Django if they were good people.

I was jealous of the dog's ability to sniff out the riffraff. If our society had Django's ability to look past physical appearances and see the real person underneath, the world would be a whole lot better place.

"You miss that rangy mutt?" I looked over at Django. He lay with his head on his paws on a cushion in the corner. He whined and wagged his tail as if he knew we were talking about him. "What about me?"

"You all right, I guess." Darling burst into laughter that turned into a coughing fit. I gave her a look. She had a heart condition, was overweight, and had only stopped smoking two years ago. She was a lot older than me, but with her unlined face, she could be anywhere between thirty and seventy. I swear, black people didn't age. Her health was a constant concern of mine. Once I tried to get her to lose weight and brought her a kale smoothie. When I put it in front of her, the look she shot me would have slayed a more sensitive person.

She tossed it in the trash, mumbling about how she wasn't going to eat "nasty ass grass juice," and how she'd lose all her "suitors" if she lost even one pound. I didn't care about any of that. All I cared about was her living a long life. When everyone you cared about died, you were finely tuned into every little possible danger sign.

"I miss you, too, D." I turned my attention back to my cards and tried to play it cool. With this hand, I could actually win. I only needed fifteen points. But Darling only needed thirteen. And she counted first. If I could hold her to twelve points I'd win. It would piss her off and ruin her night. I didn't feel a twinge of guilt. I laid down a three. There was no way she could score on that. I tried to distract her.

It is good if a warrior's enemy underestimates him during battle. A warrior must not reveal all at once if he is to prevail in war. The ability to distract one's enemy will help a warrior draw closer to victory and outmaneuver his enemy.

"What's new in the 'hood?'" I said.

Darling slapped down a five. "Eight."

She didn't answer. I looked up and locked eyes with her Pharaoh ones.

"Some deep dark shit going on."

I froze.

"People are scared," she said.

"More homeless people going missing?"

I looked at my hand. I only had one play.

"Not just homeless," Darling said. "Roscoe didn't pay rent this month. His room is empty, like he just went out the store. Left is favorite black hat. Sally lives in one of those SRO. She's up and gone. Same deal. All her stuff left behind."

"How many is that now?"

Darling leaned back, thinking. "Well, there's DannyBoy. Mr. Ed. Roscoe. Now Sally." She looked over. "That's four."

"Kato says he knows of three."

She jutted her chin at my cards.

I played my nine. "Seventeen."

She put down a seven. "Twenty-four."

"Plus, Ethel." I said.

"She was murdered, not missing."

I didn't argue. "Anyway, you look at it, it's a problem."

"Mmmm Hmmm." Darling said, taking another slug of Jack Daniels.

"What do the police say?"

Darling practically spit out her drink. "PO-lice? The police said everything is just fine, little Miss Black Woman, you run on home and don't worry your pretty little head." She shook her head. "The PO-lice. They don't care about homeless or poor people and they especially don't care about black homeless or poor people."

I threw down a three. "Twenty-seven."

"Go." She frowned I put down my other three and took my three points. Only twelve points for me to win. "Still lot of game left," I said to console her. She glowered.

"Are all those people you mentioned black?"

"Yep."

I sighed. "Kato's three missing are black, too.

"There's something evil afoot," Darling said, nodding, looking down at her cards.

"That's a fact."

"Everyone on edge. Not just because of that, either."

"I know."

The hatred in the country was growing in fervor. It didn't even seem like the country I grew up in. People were comfortable spewing vitriol and hatred like never before. Sides were being drawn in rallies and protests: self-proclaimed white nationalist groups against those seeking equality for all and many conflicts ended in bloodshed.

Last week, a protest in Oakland ended with a police car set on fire and four people beaten so bad they had to be hospitalized.

"All that stuff is heading over here," Darling said. "Today. Or tomorrow. Soon. They say them racists have some surprise planned for us here in the city. Sasha came by earlier. Said she got a tip they were holding a rally here tonight. In the plaza. She wants to write about it for the paper. I told her over my dead body. But that girl's stubborn like her mama, God rest her soul. I told her if she has to go, to take George with her."

Darling's nineteen-year-old granddaughter, Sasha, attended U.C. Berkeley and worked for the campus newspaper. George was the salon's doorman-slash-bouncer. I'd also heard the rumors. A hate group has made threats about running people of color out of the city and burning buildings down.

I scowled. "What the hell is wrong with those people?"

Darling shook her head. "No explanation for that kind of hate. It's the devil's work."

I nodded.

She flicked down a five.

I was out of cards so it was her turn to go again.

With a flourish, she smiled and dropped another five. "Ten for three."

"Go." I said, trying not to sound annoyed.

She scooped up her cards and then flipped them over as she counted them. "Fifteen-two, fifteen-four, fifteen-six, fifteen-eight and six are fourteen." She moved her peg across the finish line.

She looked at my hand laid out: four threes and a nine—and whistled.

"Damn, girl, that's a good hand," she said. "Too bad you can't count it."

"Yeah, too bad," I said, dryly. "Pretty crappy when a twenty-four hand isn't good enough." I stood and stretched. I'd never been lucky.

Django growled, lifting his head, right before the knock on the door came. Darling looked at her security camera screen and then leaned over to push a small button. The door swung open. George gestured for a small woman with a tidy black bun to come in. When Django saw it was George, he lazily wagged his tail and then put his head back on his paws. They'd already gone over all the ritualistic wiggling and face licking earlier when we arrived. Even the dog knew that with George around nobody had to worry—he could relax and go back to sleep.

George, a former linebacker with the San Francisco 49ers, was still in better shape than most of the starting lineup this year. His warm brown eyes belied his tough manner. His bald head shone in the chandelier hanging down by the door.

Stepping into the room, the woman seemed embarrassed. "Miss Darling, I'm sorry to bother you."

"It's all good, sugar. What you need?"

"My man, he got laid off last month, you know."

"Mmmm hmmm," Darling said.

"Well, the landlord comes to us this morning and says if we don't pay the rent by midnight, sheriff's office is going to be here with an eviction notice."

"Mmmm hmmm," Darling said, standing and heading toward a large desk. She fished a key on a necklace out of her ample bosom and unlocked a drawer. She withdrew a zipped black bag.

"How much you need, baby girl?"

The woman burst into tears and ran over, hugging Darling around the waist.

"Hush now. How much?"

"Eight hundred."

Darling counted out eight one-hundred-dollar bills and placed them in the woman's palm, closing her hand over the cash.

"Thank you. I promise we'll pay you back. I swear."

"Mmmm hmmm," Darling steered the woman toward the door where George waited. He took the woman's arm and the door closed behind them.

I eyed Darling as she sat back down. I stared at her until she looked up at me.

"What you looking at?"

"Last time I was here someone else came with some sob story and you forked over a small fortune then, too."

"Mmmm hmmm." She looked away.

She handed me the deck. "Loser's deal."

This time the knock was urgent. I looked over at the bank of cameras. George was outside the door alone.

Darling saw the look on his face and stood this time as she punched the button.

George was out of breath. He was holding his cell phone.

"Sasha called. They in the plaza."

Darling's face drained of color.

"Oh, sweet Jesus."

5

ACHILLES HEEL

WITHIN SECONDS, WE'D RUSHED OUT THE BACK DOOR OF THE SALON AND were running toward the Civic Center Plaza. George disappeared ahead of us. I stayed behind to match pace with Darling, who probably hadn't run since grade school recess. She kept stopping, patting her ample chest and gasping for breath.

I took her arm. "It's okay. Don't kill yourself. We're almost there. George will find Sasha."

"Oh, Lord, please keep my grandbaby safe." Darling's voice was panicked. "I told her not to get involved. I told her turn around and go straight home, back to her safe little apartment in that hippie town."

"She's just being a journalist,' I said, as we paused on one corner.

Darling dismissed my words with an irritated wave of her ringed fingers.

"I barely sleep anymore worrying about that girl. She thinks she can save the world."

Finally, after race-walking with frequent pauses, we turned the corner and caught up to George, standing on the edge of a massive crowd on his tiptoes scanning the crowd for Sasha.

The hazily lit plaza was a squirming mass of bodies. There were two distinct groups. On one side, about two hundred men, most wearing khaki pants and white polo shirts, holding Tiki torches. An order was given and almost simultaneously, all the torches were lit.

Across from this group, there were another two hundred or so people, men and women, some with dreads, some with buzz cuts, holding signs that said, "You lost the war!" and "All are welcome here!"

In between the two groups was an empty strip of concrete about ten feet wide. The two sides eyed each other warily.

Then the chanting began. The men in polo shirts yelled, "You will not replace us."

The other side yelled, "Nazis go home!"

The night was thick with anger and a strange heat. Too many bodies pressed against one another. Hatred and fear swarmed the plaza and felt almost tangible. Darling clutched my arm, her long nails digging into my flesh.

Across from us, in front of a church, a dozen clergy members locked arms and sang "Amazing Grace."

In a flurry of shouting, violence erupted. In an instant people were on each other, pushing and shoving and screaming. I tugged Darling back toward me as the crowd around us surged forward.

"There's Sasha!" she yelled, her giant eyes wide with fright. "Sasha! Sasha!"

George, who towered above us, arched his neck. "Where?"

"There!" Darling pointed one well-manicured nail. "In the pink sweatshirt."

I craned my neck but only got a glimpse of pink before the crowd swallowed her.

"I see her," George said and was gone, pushing his way through the crowd like a bulldozer, shoving people on each side of him out of the way to clear a path. For a second, I started to follow him, but the crowd quickly closed behind him and Darling clutched at my arm. I was worried about her heart. I knew there was no way she was going to leave without Sasha.

Smoke filled the air and popping sounds echoed off the

surrounding buildings. It didn't sound like gunshots, but I wasn't sure. I also heard the chopping of a helicopter high above.

Right in front of us, three men in polo shirts had another man on the ground, kicking him in the ribs. When one man wound up to kick him in the head, I had my hand inside my jacket on my gun. I was about to step in when a young man with a lumberjack beard yanked the attacker away. Then those two were at each other, punching and kicking and clawing. Droplets of blood scattered through the air like they'd been flung by a sprinkler.

I dragged Darling by the arm and pulled her several feet away from the angry mob and blood spatter, where she crumpled softly onto the lawn bordering the plaza.

"Oh, my Lord. Jesus help us." She was quivering.

I stood and she grabbed my hand. "Stay with me, Gia."

Sitting back down I threw my arm around her. I'd never seen Darling afraid of anything. The biggest, baddest drug dealer in the Tenderloin had held a gun to her head and she had laughed in his face.

But Sasha was her Achilles heel.

More popping noises erupted and more screams. Smoke filled the air.

At the end of the plaza, a line of police officers stood with their arms crossed. Some held shields. All wore tactical gear and masks. They were not moving. They were keeping the fight contained so it wouldn't spill out onto Polk Street. But they were doing nothing to intervene. I was outraged.

If those in power fail to protect the weak, it is up to the warrior to step in and see that the vulnerable are protected.

I glared at the police and then patted Darling's arm. "It's okay. George is probably with her right now."

I glanced over at the roiling mass and hoped I was right.

———

AFTER A FEW MINUTES of sitting with Darling, another friend of hers came over, panting.

"Miss Darling, you okay?"

"I'm fine, honey. It's Sasha. You seen her?" She pressed her lips tightly together.

"No, ma'am." The woman who had her hair pulled back tightly in braids and wore a tank top and shorts flopped down on the grass. "Hope she got out of there. Those people are crazy."

"Mmmm hmmm," Darling said.

Any trace of the terror she had showed me earlier was gone. The big bad strong woman was back. I was relieved. I didn't know how to handle Darling falling apart.

Now that someone was there to sit with her, I couldn't wait any longer. I leaned down. "You sit here with Darling until I come back, or else take her to Katrina's and buy her a stiff drink." I peeled off a one-hundred-dollar bill. "And some food." I peeled off another bill. "And buy yourself something, too."

Without waiting for an answer, I slipped into the crowd. I was shoved here and there and had to hop over a body or two on the ground, but I kept my elbows out and headed toward where I'd last seen George's bald head.

My gun felt like it was alive in my shoulder holster, but I knew taking it out would be a game changer in a game I wasn't even playing.

6

BILLY CLUB

I WAS NEARLY ACROSS THE PLAZA WHEN I SAW A GROUP CROUCHED DOWN around a man. My heart raced. George. I pushed and shoved my way through. "Get out of my way!" I shouted.

With terror streaking through me, I knelt down by George's head. A huge gash sliced through his temple. He was unconscious, his long black eyelashes closed. "Call 911. Get an ambulance here now. Call 911. Now. What are you waiting for?" I shouted to the knot of people surrounding us.

When I finally looked up, I saw they were all staring at me. One man in Elvis Costello glasses cleared his throat. "We already did."

I stood and looked around.

"We need a doctor! Is there a doctor anywhere? Help, we need a doctor!"

The crowd in the plaza had thinned. A large mass of people streamed toward Market Street, a roiling group of anger and hatred and frustration. The only people who remained in the plaza were straggling groups nursing the injured.

I ripped off my leather jacket and folded it up, gently sliding it under George's head.

He groaned. I took that as a good sign. I leaned down and

murmured in his ear, "It's going to be okay, George, you hang in there. It's going to be okay. It's going to be okay."

A man in a blazer and glasses leaned down beside me.

"I'm a doctor. An ambulance is on the way."

That's when I remembered. Sasha. I turned to the group surrounding George.

"There was a girl. He was trying to get to her. She is about five-foot-two and was wearing a pink sweatshirt."

Blank faces.

"I saw her." A woman stepped forward. She had shoulder-length curly blond hair and a beauty mark above her full lips. She wore a faded T-shirt with Bob Marley's smiling face on it, baggy jeans, and purple Converse high tops. "They took her. A few minutes ago."

"What? Who took her?"

"A group of men. Those ones that wear masks."

"The group Anonymous? The ones who wear Guy Fawkes' masks?"

Another man in a goatee stepped forward. "No, these guys were dressed all in black and had black masks on."

"You've got to be fucking kidding me." Terror streaked through me.

"They were dragging her by the arms. She was crying and screaming. Your friend here tried to stop them and they hit him in the head," the woman said.

"With a Billy club," someone added.

"Jesus."

The man in the goatee looked down. "When they took this fellow down, we were too afraid to try to stop them. There were too many of them."

"It's okay." Inside, though, I was thinking it was not okay. Not at all. "Why did they grab her? I don't understand."

The woman with the curly hair spoke again. "Because she was a reporter. They walked up to her and she showed them some badge or something around her neck and I heard her say she was a reporter. And she was holding a notebook and pen."

That sounded about right.

"Fuck me."

In the distance, the wail of ambulances sounded closer. I tried to squash the panic rising in my throat. "Where did you last see them? Where were they taking her?"

"Down Fulton. About five minutes ago."

Right before I arrived.

Two paramedics raced up and knelt by George. There was nothing I could do for him now. I turned and sprinted toward Fulton Street.

As I passed the Pioneer Monument—a life-size statue of Minerva, the goddess of war—I murmured a plea to her. "I could use some of your help right about now."

With the San Francisco Library on my right and the Asian Art Museum on my left, I crossed Hyde Street and ended up in another plaza, the United Nations Plaza. My breath was ragged and I wheezed a little. I needed to quit smoking pot. And cigarettes.

This plaza was eerily deserted.

But at the far end, where the plaza met the end of Leavenworth Street by the Art Institute, I saw something. A dark huddled mass. It parted and I caught a glimpse of pink.

Sasha.

I darted toward them, keeping to the shadows cast by trees lining the plaza. As I got closer, an SUV pulled up near the group. Two of the dark figures holding Sasha dragged her toward the vehicle. She struggled, but wasn't screaming. I saw a strip of white across her mouth.

Reaching under my sweatshirt into the holster inside my waistband attached to my belt, I lifted out my Beretta Nano 9mm. I kept it by my side as I ran. I was only a half block away when someone opened the SUV door. Then all of them piled into the vehicle, hauling Sasha with them.

"Sasha!" I screamed. For one second, it seemed as if something would happen and then the SUV screeched away.

I chased it toward Market Street, getting a glimpse of part of its license plate. 6LIK. It crossed Market Street at probably thirty miles an hour. There was no way I could keep up on foot. A man in a silver Mercedes pulled up beside me, oblivious to what was going on. He had his window down and was tapping his fingers on the steering wheel, singing along to some Caribbean music.

I leaned over and stuck the muzzle of my Beretta in the window.

"Get out. Now. I won't hurt you. This is an emergency. A life or death situation." I said hoarsely, out of breath from running.

He refused to look at me, the whites of his eyes staring straight ahead, hands clutching the steering wheel.

"Did you hear me?" I said. "I need your car. Now. A girl's life is in danger. Get out."

A BART train drowned out my words as it screeched by in front of me, blocking my way and making sure I had zero chance of following the SUV.

I lowered my gun. "Never mind," I said. "Sorry to bother you."

The man kept staring straight ahead.

I put my gun back in its holster and turned back toward the plaza.

7

BLUE VELVET

WHEN I GOT BACK TO THE PLAZA ONLY A FEW STRAGGLERS ROAMED IN the dark. George was gone. The police had left. The spot where I'd left Darling on the lawn was empty.

A group of people my age huddled at the edge on the lawn, passing around a bottle and a joint.

"Do you mind?" I held out my hand.

A guy with a man bun handed me the bottle. I chugged some, handed it back and wiped my mouth with the back of my palm. A girl offered me the joint, but I shook my head and walked away.

When I got to Polk Street, I took out my cell phone. When I'd been running, it had been vibrating in my pocket nonstop. Twelve missed calls from Darling.

"Thank God," she said when she picked up. "I can't get ahold of anybody. They said it was over but Sasha's not answering her phone. George isn't either."

"You somewhere safe?"

"What aren't you telling me?" Her voice was suddenly low and dangerous. "You talk to me right now."

I was worried about her heart, but I couldn't lie.

"They took her, Darling."

"What?" She gasped. "My grandbaby? They took my grandbaby?"

"I tried to stop them. They took her because she was a reporter. They left in a black SUV. They knocked George out to get to her. He's at the hospital. We need to call the police."

Silence.

"Meet me at Katrina's," she said and hung up.

————

WHEN I WALKED into Katrina's, the entire place glowed. White candles covered every surface. An elaborately ornate metal trellis covered one wall, designed purely to hold dozens of candles.

My motorcycle boots were silent on the black marble floors. I passed the blue velvet booth with the engraved metal plate that said "Gia Santella." Darling sat, surrounded, at a circular table in the corner. Her reflection multiplied into infinity by gigantic silver-framed mirrors covering two walls.

As I got to the table, everybody but Darling moved to another table.

"Sit." Her voice was deadly. I swallowed and obeyed. A man in black pulled heavy purple satin curtains around the table, closing the two of us off from the rest of the world.

As soon as the curtains closed, Darling's shoulders slumped and she put her head down.

"They kidnapped Sasha. We need to call the police."

She lifted her head, tossing her curls.

"The PO-lice? We aren't bringing in the PO-lice. You think they give a shit about a little black girl gone missing in a protest? Nuh uh. They don't care."

I wanted to argue with her, but I couldn't. I didn't know if she was right or wrong. I hadn't grown up black in the Bay Area. I thought about it for a second.

"I'll pay for the best private investigator in the country."

"Nope."

Raising an eyebrow, I waited. She clamped her lips together, her huge Egyptian eyes staring me down. She wasn't budging.

"What?"

"You."

"What about me?"

"You find Sasha."

It took me a second to absorb that. "Darling, you know I'd do anything to help you, but I'm not a detective. I'm not a P.I. We need experts to help us find her."

"You found out who killed your mama and pop, didn't you?"

"That's different."

Darling crossed her arms across her large bust. "Is it?"

"Yes! They were dead! If I messed up, they would still be dead!"

Darling stared me down again.

I kept trying. "Sasha is out there somewhere. If the police know she's missing, they can spread the word, put it on the news, do all sorts of things to help find her."

"I don't trust the police. I don't trust nobody else getting in my business. You know my business, Gia."

I couldn't argue with that. "But they are our best bet to find Sasha."

I waited for her to argue. She closed her eyes. When she opened them, her gaze was pure steel.

"Gia, you know me. You know how I love my grandbaby. If I thought there was a snowball's chance in hell of the police finding my baby I would do anything, give up everything to make sure she was safe." She threw back her shoulders. "Sure, there are good police. I know that. Probably more good ones than bad. But when it comes to my grandbaby, my life, I can't afford to take a chance that one of the other ones is in charge."

She leaned over and grabbed my hand.

"I need you to find her."

A mixture of despair, helplessness, and fury shot through me. Mother fucker. I was going to have to agree, but it didn't mean I had to pretend to be happy about it.

"Fuck. Fuck. Fuck." I shook my head. She stared. "Fine. Are you happy? Fine."

"Just promise me, you'll try." She sat back, relaxed now. Of course, she was. She'd gotten her goddamn way. As usual.

"I still think it's a mistake. Just so you know." I glared at her. What gave her such confidence in a fuck up like me, I'd never know.

Darling sat back and snapped her fingers.

The curtains pulled open.

Within seconds, the booth was filled again with Darling's friends and platters of Katrina's famous comfort food arrived: meatloaf, mashed potatoes, roast beef slices, gravy, biscuits, creamed corn, even tater tot hot dish. Katrina's catered to all the transplants to San Francisco who missed down home cooking and wanted a break from the city's latest trendy fusion cuisine.

I picked at the tater tots and sipped my whiskey. I was still pissed off at Darling and nearly sick to my stomach with the thought that it was up to me to find Sasha. My mind raced, trying to latch on to a starting point. I wanted to race back to the plaza to find the woman with the curly blond hair who saw Sasha's kidnappers, but I knew she wasn't there anymore. The TV screen hanging above the bar, showed the mayor addressing reporters in the empty plaza. Even so, I searched the crowd around him for a blond. I was kicking myself for not getting her name or contact information. She was the only lead I had.

Except one. I had the partial license plate number: 6LIK.

Mayor John Evans was flanked by a bunch of cops in tactical gear.

Figures he was there. His re-election platform focused on making the city safer, specifically the Tenderloin. His slogan was "Our city can kick crime's ass." A riff on Rudy Giuliani's "Our city can kick your city's ass" or something. Not quite as obnoxious. Almost, though.

However, tonight's violence wasn't good for his mayoral run. The only ass kicking was going to be his. The news ticker at the bottom of the screen said, "At least a dozen injured in conflict at Civic Center Plaza."

The broadcast cut to aerial footage of the square. I sat up straight.

Maybe it would show the men who took Sasha. But I didn't see anything during the brief clip. It was Channel 5. I was sure they had more footage than just what they aired.

Lost deep in thought, the hairs on the back of my neck prickled. Across the room, a man with startling pale skin was watching me. A fedora was pulled low on his forehead. Something about him seemed otherworldly, like he was a vampire, even though I didn't believe in that sort of crap. He was thin and too tall somehow. Too big for the space, like he needed to duck even though the ceilings at Katrina's were ten-feet tall. Something was odd about his eyes. At the same time, he seemed familiar. It was right there on the edge of my memory why that was, but the knowledge slipped away at the same time he stepped out the side door.

Instinctively, I rose to follow him, but then sat back down. He hadn't done anything. Being a weirdo wasn't a good enough reason for me to chase after a stranger. If that were my criteria, I'd be chasing after nut jobs all the live long day.

Darling nudged me. "We're going to the hospital to see George."

I stood. When our group reached the door, we found ourselves facing Mayor Evans and his entourage. The mayor wore an overcoat, cashmere blazer, and jeans that looked like they had been ironed. His graying hair was slightly mussed and one bushy gray eyebrow was askew. I'd never seen him look anything but perfectly coiffed. Like he'd been yanked out of bed for the press conference.

Standing in front of Darling, the mayor dipped his head, a stray gray lock bobbing. "Ms. Fitzgerald."

"Mayor Evans." Darling raised an eyebrow and the mayor stepped aside, letting us pass.

Outside, a line of black cars waited for us. I shivered. Fog was rolling down the street. It was headed our way. People piled into the black cars until I was alone on the sidewalk. I was still pissed off at Darling. How dare her turn to me in something so serious? I knew I was being childish. What else was knew?

Darling poked her head out of the back seat of the first car and gestured for me to join her.

Once we were alone inside the dark interior, she leaned back in her seat and closed her eyes. After a few seconds, I did the same. My anger seeped out of me, replaced by anxiety and fear. It was too much pressure. I leaned forward and put my head in my hands. Darling was making a mistake counting on me.

———

AT THE HOSPITAL, Darling and I stood over George's hospital bed. He was still unconscious and had so many damn tubes stuck in him I wanted to punch something. I barely knew the dude, but nobody, nobody, deserved to be beaten like this. His face was a swollen mess and a huge bandage took up most of his once regal bald head.

I went to grab coffee for us in the cafeteria downstairs, trying to give Darling a moment alone with George. When I came back, Darling had pulled up a chair beside his bed and was holding his hand. A nurse came in holding the leather jacket that I'd put under George's head. Darling gave her a look and the nurse handed the jacket to me.

I shrugged it on and walked out. In the waiting room, I sat with some of Darling's fan club members or whoever they were. Her posse. They regarded me warily. They didn't like that some dumb white girl was their mentor's closest ally right now. I didn't blame them. But Darling and I shared a bond that transcended everything else that made us different. That's why I knew I would do anything to find Sasha.

We all sat there in silence until Darling came out.

"Any change?"

She shook her head. I sighed.

"I'm staying the night," she said.

"I'm going home. Think Django will be okay at your place tonight?" Hopefully he was still in her back room.

"Mmm Hmm." Darling was distracted. "I had Shelley feed him and take him for a walk while we were at Katrina's." Shelley was her manager at the salon and her assistant in all things.

I was about to leave when Darling grabbed my arm. Hard. She leaned over and whispered in my ear. "You find my grandbaby, you hear?"

I didn't answer, just stared at her until she let go of my arm.

As the elevator door closed with me inside, I kicked the wall. I was one hundred percent royally, truly, and thoroughly fucked.

8

BARBED WIRE

THE NEXT MORNING, I WOKE EARLY AND LEFT MY APARTMENT WHILE THE fog was still thick on the ground. I needed to go get Django, but first I wanted to check out the plaza again in case there were any clues.

As I crossed Bush Street I made my way quickly through Tenderloin Heights. Before long, I was in the Sit/Lie neighborhood. Homeless people tucked into old sleeping bags or sat propped on cardboard boxes despite the mayor's new "Sit/Lie" city law prohibiting people from sitting or lying down on sidewalks or other public spaces.

Most people in the Tenderloin saw the law for what it was: a way to discriminate against the homeless. In Berkeley, the city was friendlier to the homeless and allowed them to sit or lie between seven in the morning and ten at night.

As I walked, the fog grew thicker, making me feel disoriented. By now I should've been to Market Street, but instead was on a street that was eerily deserted. No shops. No apartments. Only buildings that seemed abandoned. I jumped when a man stumbled out of the fog before me. He mumbled something incoherent before stumbling off in another direction.

A patch of fog cleared and a massive building loomed before me.

A twelve-foot-high chain link fence capped with barbed wire surrounded the building's adjacent parking lot. All the windows were boarded up. Despite the desolation, I got the feeling I was being watched. I hurried away, without looking back.

Maybe it was my upbringing—my nana had been extraordinarily suspicious—but I believed that some places emanated evil. That a building could be infused with dark things. Even abandoned and empty like the one I'd just passed.

All my life I'd been able to sense this darkness in places. As a little kid, I thought that everybody could.

Sometimes when I was really little we would go into an old restaurant and I would kick and scream and say I wasn't going to eat there. Over the years my parents grew to expect my odd sensory reaction to certain places and tolerated it, even indulged it, by not making me go places that I said made me feel uncomfortable. As I grew older, I realized others didn't share my feelings about places.

One day, my mother took me shopping on Melrose Avenue in Los Angeles. I was thirteen, gangly and awkward and desperate to be cool and accepted by my classmates in Monterey. After growing up watching Melrose Place, I knew this was where all the cool kids shopped.

I spotted a small store on the second floor of a building that had a cool T-shirt in the window. My mother was talking on the phone to my dad so she waited on the sidewalk while I went upstairs.

The minute I opened the door, a clammy oppressive feeling overcame me and I was suddenly ice cold. The only sound was the chimes on the door echoing behind me. The store was darker than I expected and jam packed. While there were a few clothing items hanging up here and there, most of the store was taken up by candles, vials of oils, and small boxes and books all displayed on antique dressers with mirrors. The air smelled dank but also like some heady perfume that seemed to overtake every other sense.

"Hello?"

Nobody answered. I saw a light coming from a doorway at the back. Every fiber of my being told me to get out of there, but I really wanted to see the turquoise T-shirt in the window. As I made my way over to it, I passed a small display on a black-painted dresser.

I glanced over and my heart stopped. A petrified hand lay in a red satin-lined box in the center of the dresser. I stood staring at it. Confused.

Then with the smallest movement of air I felt something. The dresser's mirror showed a woman in a turban standing at my shoulder. I screamed and ran out of the store, her laughter trailing behind me

Down on the sidewalk, I breathlessly told my mother about the hand.

"Let's go see about that." I loved that about my mother. She took me seriously. And wasn't afraid of anything.

Reluctantly, I trailed behind her up the stairs. When we walked in, it was as if I had entered a different store. It was bright and cheery. The woman in the turban was whistling and there was something pleasant playing on a radio.

"*Bon jour!*" the woman said. "Welcome to my shop. Are you looking for something in particular?"

I stared at her dumbfounded.

My mother smiled. "Oh, my daughter was just in here and saw something she wanted to show me."

"Yes. She ran out before I had a chance to help her."

I glared at the woman.

"Over there," I said, nudging my mother.

My mother casually walked over to the black-painted dresser. As we drew closer, I saw a sign that I either hadn't noticed or that hadn't been there before "Check out our new Halloween decorations."

I scrunched up my face. The sign was new. I would've noticed it before. I was sure.

As we got closer, I looked at the red satin-lined box. There was a hand in it. A fake, pink plastic hand with red-painted nails. My mother picked it up, holding it in her palm for a few seconds before putting it back.

I turned and ran out the door.

A few seconds later, my mother joined me on the sidewalk.

"She changed it." I said, anger surging through me. "Mama, it was a real hand. It was like a mummy, all shriveled up. She must have switched it when I left."

A strange look crossed my mother's face. One I'd never seen before.

"Gia, back in the old country, there were things that some of the women could see. It was a gift. It was something that helped keep people safe. You have that gift. You always have. I want you to always, always listen to that feeling. It is real. Even if—" she glanced up at the second story. "Even if, someone tries to trick you and make you believe that what you see or feel is not real. It is. It is as real as me and you. Don't ever doubt."

I hugged her so tight I couldn't breathe. I might have sniffled a little.

"Let's go now and find you some *tres chic* clothing." She grabbed my hand. I usually was embarrassed by her affection in public, but right then I held on tightly.

As we walked away, I cast one last glance back at the store. The turbaned woman was standing in the window, stock-still, staring.

The building in the Tenderloin was the first time in a long while that I'd had that ominous feeling of pervasive dread and danger. I knew without a doubt that people had died there and died terribly. It wasn't too much of a stretch. The Tenderloin— along with a storied history of speakeasies, burlesque houses, jazz clubs, and brothels—was also renowned for its high crime rate. Today, the crime, the bars, strip clubs, and single-occupancy hotel rooms all remained, along with an entire small village of homeless people.

As I emerged from the fog onto Market Street, I spotted Jack-O pushing his shopping cart along and whistling. He had on painter's pants and about three flannel plaid shirts layered upon one another. His whiskers were gray and only a few tufts of brown hair behind his ears remained on his head.

"Oh, Gia!" He doffed an imaginary hat at me.

"Jack-O, just the man I'm looking for." I hadn't realized it until the words came out of my mouth, but it was true.

"Oh, what can I do for you on this fine morning?" He gave me a missing-tooth grin.

"Fine morning?"

He laughed. "Okay, it's cold, but I woke up this morning and I'm still alive, so it's a fine day."

"I'll give you that," I said and then my smile disappeared. "I need your help. I need you to spread the word on the streets. I'm looking for a girl. She's about five-foot-two, black straight hair, wearing a pink sweatshirt."

"White girl?"

"Nah. Black."

Jack-O grew serious, listening and nodding.

"Men in masks grabbed her last night at the protest."

"Oh, boy," Jack-O said and shook his head.

"If you can find anyone who saw anything, I'd be very grateful. Tell them I'll make it worth their while if the info is good. The men put her in the back of an SUV over on Leavenworth near Market Street. I only caught a partial plate: 6LIK. If they can find me that vehicle, same deal, I'll make it worthwhile."

"Oh. 6LIK?" Jack-O said. "Got it. I'm on it, Gia."

"Thanks. You can always get messages to me at Darling's."

"You sure you don't want to move into Swanson Place?" I'd tried to talk him into it before. Many of the homeless people I spoke to in the Tenderloin wanted to remain on the streets for reasons I couldn't fathom, talking about freedom and so on. But others told me they were waiting for that one break that would lift them off the streets. Swanson Place was my plan to give them that break. I already had a clipboard with ten names on it and had promised all ten of them a spot in the new building along with employment downstairs.

"Oh. Nah, I appreciate the offer, but this is my home. I don't want to go to the Sunset."

"It's not that far away ..."

He turned to leave.

"You need money for breakfast or something?" It was a dumb question and I immediately regretted saying it.

He didn't answer, only swallowed and looked away.

I leaned over and handed him two twenties. "This is for helping me spread the word about the girl. I appreciate it."

He didn't say anything but the money disappeared up his long sleeve.

I turned and walked away before I embarrassed either one of us any more than I already had.

9

MRS. ROBIN HOOD

DJANGO PRACTICALLY KNOCKED ME DOWN IN HIS EXCITEMENT TO see me.

"Good boy." I laughed and patted him. The damn dog acted like I'd been gone a year instead of only overnight. He kept jumping on my nice jeans and slobbering all over me.

Darling smiled at me, but I could tell the fight had gone out of her.

"Nothing from Sasha?"

"Not a word." For the first time, Darling actually looked like someone who could have a granddaughter. She had slight bags under her eyes and there were other small signs that something was off. There was something about the set of her mouth. Her thick black curls were a masterpiece, as usual, but her silk shirt was a little bit wrinkled and there was a slight unevenness in her application of lip liner. But overall, she still looked pretty damn put together. Something I couldn't manage on my best day.

"George?"

"Same."

I shook my head. Then I walked over to Darling's galley kitchen, poured us some coffee and dumped a shot of Bailey's Irish Cream into each one. "Sit down a second. I've got an idea I need to run by you."

We both settled into the leather couches and sipped our coffees. On the walk over, I had thought carefully about how I was going to approach this one.

Gingerly.

Darling probably distrusted police for good reason. I knew nothing about that, but I did know at least one San Francisco police officer I thought we could trust. James.

Okay. Truth is, I slept with him. A few times. For a while I was sort of freaking out about him because I knew there was a chance I could fall for him and that was the last thing I had in mind. Of course, as usual, I single-handedly destroyed any chance of a normal, healthy relationship when I did my "thing" around him. My fucked-up "thing" to keep people away.

Being distant. Drinking too much. Smoking pot. Mouthy AF.

The first time I lit up, when we walked outside a North Beach restaurant after dinner, he looked like I'd slapped him.

"Gia! I'm a cop!"

"I know!" I said smiling. One reason he was so damn sexy. Body toned to perfection. Smooth and sexy mocha skin. Cheekbones for days. Add a uniform and gun belt? *Mama mia!*

"You're smoking pot." He ran a hand across his head and scowled.

"So?" I said, waving my joint around in front of him. "Hello! Prop 64 passed!"

"You're standing on the sidewalk."

I lifted my eyebrow. "I just want a little toke after that amazing linguine."

"It's against the law to smoke on the sidewalk."

"Against the law like go to jail or against the law like slap on the wrist?" I exhaled over his head and then regretted it when I saw a flash of anger in his eyes.

"Either way, I'm a cop. Have a little respect."

"Hmmm." I thought about it. I wasn't sure it was disrespectful to smoke marijuana in front of a police officer. He turned away, but I could tell by the set of his shoulders he was pissed. He whirled around, started to say something, and then swore.

"You've got to be kidding me," he said, looking over my shoulder. "Is that a school right there? Oh, shit. It is. Put that out, right now, Gia. You could really get me in trouble. What if one of my supervisors drove by right now?"

"School's out, James." I couldn't hide the annoyance in my voice. What a buzz kill. I dropped the joint on the sidewalk and stepped on it with the toe of my boot as I walked away. He followed me in silence.

When we got back to my place, he didn't come in.

"Is it that bad that I like to smoke pot?" I asked. Staring at his mouth, I realized I could give up marijuana for that.

He crossed his arms over his chest. "It's all of it."

"All of what?" I picked at some leftover red fingernail polish on my thumb. "I don't get it."

"I think you do get it and that's the problem." The way he looked at me made me squirm. I could see the writing on the wall. He was dumping me. Frankly, it was a first for me. I usually beat them to the punch. I glared at the doorman lingering nearby, a little too interested in our driveway conversation. I turned back, but James had already walked away. He slammed the door of his Saab and drove off. He drove so slowly I wondered if he was going to turn around and come back, but his tail lights soon disappeared. It wouldn't have hurt so much if he had peeled out. At least then I would've know there was some emotion and passion involved.

It felt like he'd made a very logical and rational decision to dump me.

Which is what it was.

This was before I met my sort-of-boyfriend Bobby. Bobby made me forget all about James. Bobby was the opposite of James physically—less G.I. Joe and more surfer-slash-skater boy with molten hazel eyes and tawny hair that fell nearly to his shoulders.

I'd pushed all thoughts of James out of my life when I started seeing Bobby a few months ago. But every once in a while, my body remembered. It happened when I caught a glimpse of a guy from behind with the same physique or spotted a profile with a similar jawline to James. I must admit, though, I did binge watch a few episodes of "Criminal Minds" the other night because James reminds me of Shemar Moore.

Now, with Darling's strong anti-cop stance, I figured James was the only upstanding guy I could vouch for in the San Francisco Police Department. I just needed to convince Darling.

I spilled it all to Darling and poured us more spiked coffee.

She downed hers before she spoke.

"I don't know, Gia."

"Darling, I know police have done you wrong, but you know better than to stereotype an entire population of people. There are good and bad people in every group. You said so yourself."

We sat there in awkward silence.

Finally, I said something. "Django! You're putting my foot to sleep!" He was sitting on my foot like I was going to leave him again, which I was.

Then, she gave in.

"Okay, Gia." She said it with a big sigh. "You can talk to him. It's against my better judgement. I hope you aren't making a mistake."

"I'm not," I said. But I didn't quite believe it.

"And Gia? I don't want him nosing around up in my business. Tell him all that is off limits. You understand?"

"Absolutely." I said it, but a flicker of doubt ran through me. James *was* upstanding and a good guy, which made me worry that he wouldn't let anything illegal slide. I'd have to make the ground rules clear when I went begging for help.

"I'll be back for this big baby in about an hour." I jutted my chin at Django, trying to avoid looking at his sad, accusing eyes as I walked out.

A small part of me was nervous when I got to the precinct steps. We hadn't parted on the best terms and for some reason I felt like by talking to James I was betraying Bobby, which was absurd.

Bobby and I had no commitment to one another. Besides that, I was turning to James for help, not awesomely mind-blowing sex.

Well, good, then. This would be a test. It would prove whether I was a heartless slut like I feared or whether I was capable of being a good, sort-of-part-time, long-distance girlfriend to Bobby. I'd had plenty of opportunities to sleep around since Bobby and I started regularly seeing each other a few months ago, but so far, I hadn't even been tempted. Not for a second. But ... in this case, with James, I knew what was under the hood. Oh boy, did I know.

I took a deep breath and tugged on the glass door of the police substation.

———

THE RECEPTIONIST at the precinct said James would be out in a few minutes and I could take a seat. But it took him thirty. By the time he opened the door, I was half asleep. But as soon as I saw him, my heart beat double time. He had on his police uniform: tight blue pants and a blue shirt. Ever since I first met him, no matter how hard I tried, I couldn't ditch the image of him in that uniform dancing to something throbbing and low, twirling his handcuffs, slowly, tantalizing, unbuttoning his clothes ...

When we were together, he'd been more than willing to experiment in the bedroom. But to my everlasting chagrin, he'd always refused to play bad cop with me.

"Gia?" His forehead scrunched. I guess I'd been staring.

He really was a specimen. All that time in the gym sure paid off. I stood quickly, rubbing my palms on my pants. "Do you have a second?"

"Sure. Come on back." He seemed wary, guarded, and distant. Not like someone whose tongue had traced a path across every inch of my body.

The door to the lobby slammed closed behind us, making me feel claustrophobic. He headed down a long hallway and didn't wait to see if I was keeping up. Fine by me. It gave me a good view of his remarkably firm ass.

He turned into a doorway so quickly I nearly stumbled. He flicked on the lights and waited by the door for me to come into the window-less room.

"Have a seat." His voice was clinical. Not a trace of warmth.

When I pulled up a chair at the small table, he shut the door and pulled out a chair across from me.

"Is this where you interrogate the crooks?" I said. I smiled, trying to lighten the tension.

He waited a few seconds chewing his inner lip before he answered in a dull voice. "Yes."

I swallowed. Nobody acted like this unless they'd been hurt. It was obvious now.

"I'm really sorry about the way things ended," I said, wincing a little. "Sometimes I do stupid things like that. Act badly when I start to care about someone. I'd like to apologize. I'm really sorry. Not just that night, but that whole week." I clamped my lips together. It was way more than I intended to spill when I opened my mouth and it was so raw and revealing I felt like I was going to vomit. But it felt right. I knew I needed to say it. Every word.

He swallowed, his Adam's apple bobbing. "Thank you."

We both sat there in silence. I felt like an asshole.

Finally, he stood and headed toward the door. He turned to me. "Is that all?"

I shook my head.

"Did you come here simply to apologize?"

"I should've come solely to apologize, you're right." God, I was such a jerk. "And I should've come a lot sooner. But the truth is I came because I need your help. You're the only cop I can trust."

He sat back down and folded his hands together. He wasn't giving me an inch.

I launched into it: Darling and Sasha and the protesters and the partial license plate number. He sat silent.

"I'm hoping you might help. Discreetly," I added at the end. "As I mentioned, my friend, she's good people, James. Really, really good people. She takes care of those in need. She would do anything for anyone. But some of what she does to finance that isn't all above-board. She would never be involved in anything illegal that would hurt someone else, like distributing drugs or prostitution or anything like that. But she's got this business, involving, let's just say paperwork and documents that really, actually helps people. She won't just give stuff to anyone. If you're a thug or a low life, forget about it. But if you are down and out and need help, like say, you're an abused woman with a husband who is going to kill you ... she can help you disappear. She's like Robin Hood. Like Mrs. Robin Hood."

I spilled it all in one big rush, my words falling over themselves.

He was chewing on the inside of his lip and his eyes were narrowed. He still hadn't said word one. I was waiting, holding my breath.

Finally, he nodded.

"What does that mean?" I asked. "Yes? You'll help?"

"Gia, you do realize I'm a beat cop. A street cop. I'm not a detective."

"Not *yet*," I said, playing my card. He'd talked about working his way up to detective. "Maybe this can be your big break?"

"More like it would get me kicked off the force."

I raised an eyebrow and frowned.

"I can't operate without my supervisors knowing about this," he said. "I'm not the type of dude who goes rogue, Gia. You know that. Unlike you, I'm a rule follower."

I let the dig go. Besides it was the truth.

"You can't go to your supervisor with this." I remembered how firm Darling was on this. "We just need a little help. Not much. Just a little search of the DMV database. Believe me if I could search that license plate on my own I would've left you out of this."

James bit his lip and looked off over my shoulder.

"Please," I was begging now. "It's a young woman's life possibly in danger."

"Possibly? Now I really think I should go to my sergeant."

"You can't. Please."

He crossed his arms over his chest and shook his head. He was clearly frustrated. I waited and watched. Then he sighed.

"Give me the partial plate number."

I slid a small scrap of paper over to him.

He stood and opened the door. "You have forty-eight hours."

"What?"

"If she's not back by six p.m. on Sunday, I'm taking this to my sergeant."

"No, you can't." I stood.

He handed the paper back to me. "Those are my terms."

I crossed my arms and refused to take it back. "Fine." I glared at him and he left, the door closing behind him.

10

PURPLE RAIN

THE DRIVE ACROSS THE BAY BRIDGE WAS SURPRISINGLY PAINLESS. MOST of the traffic was heading into the city while I was heading out. I called Darling on my way.

"I'm heading to Sasha's to ask some questions. You okay keeping Django for a while?"

"He my dog now. He loves me more than you. I'm gonna keep him."

"Ha ha," I said, but a part of me worried. He *did* love Darling. A lot.

Then Darling grew serious.

"You find my grandbaby, Gia."

Sasha's apartment in Berkeley was tucked up in the hills near a cool old movie theater that was showing *Wings of Desire*. Sasha's small bungalow was tucked off the street and down a small path crowded with bushes and trees.

The door was painted blue. I knocked until a girl with long stringy hair wearing big flannel pants and a U.C. T-shirt opened the door. Her eyes were barely open behind thick glasses.

"Are you Raya?"

"You Sasha's grandma's friend?"

"Yes." I was relieved. Darling must have warned the girl I was coming.

"Did you find Sasha?" Her voice cracked. It was then I noticed her eyes were red and puffy from crying.

"Not yet."

She stood there dazed.

"Can I come in?"

The living room was the size of my closet and was crowded with a couch, TV, and one armchair. Books were piled on the coffee table and a tall palm stood in one corner. Everything was neat and tidy. I followed the girl down the hall into the kitchen where a small table with three chairs was also piled with books.

She flopped into one of the chairs. A doorway off the kitchen showed a small hall with three doors.

"Sasha's room is the one on the right."

A small twin bed took up most of the room. The bed was made with a flowered duvet. Filmy lavender curtains covered the window. A "Purple Rain" poster was taped above the bed. Across from the bed was a small desk that looked like command central. It had bookshelves above it and filing cabinets on each side.

On the desk was a picture of Sasha and her mother, Meredith, who died a few years ago of breast cancer. I stared at it. I'd only met Sasha once at the salon, but remembered she had the most mesmerizing eyes. It felt like she could see right through you.

She had her grandmother's regal nose and cheekbones and burnished bronze skin. But now that I saw her beside her mother in the photo, I knew where Sasha got her black flashing eyes.

I picked up the picture. Her mother was already fighting cancer at the time the picture was taken, but her eyes sparkled with life from underneath the stylish fisherman's cap she wore with long dangly earrings. Her full red lips pulled back into a brilliant smile. I'd never had the pleasure of meeting her. I met Darling shortly after when I first moved to San Francisco. Darling and I became fast friends, bonded in our grief. Mine over my mother and father. Hers over her daughter.

I took a picture of the photo so I could show it to people around the Tenderloin.

Sasha's bookshelves revealed her passions and intelligence: Carl Bernstein and Bob Woodward's "All the President's Men" sat between Stephen Hawking's "A Brief History of Time" and Maya Angelou's "I Know Why the Caged Bird Sings."

The desk had a big empty spot in the middle. A small U.C. coffee mug held pencils and pens. A tiny upright dresser no wider than me held her lingerie, underwear, socks, and pajamas. No diary or journal tucked into the folds of clothes.

The small closet was jam-packed with clothes. A stack of shoe-boxes was on the floor. I flipped each lid to see if they contained anything but shoes, but struck out.

Then I tackled the bookshelves, idly flipping through books looking for scraps of paper to fall out. Nothing. Then, the filing cabinets.

Sasha, a sophomore at school, was extremely organized. She had files labeled for stories she wanted to write for the campus newspaper, files labeled for her classes, her assignments, her resumes, newspapers she wanted to work for when she graduated, a file for bills to be paid, one for bills paid, and one for fashion. I was relieved to see at least one file that showed she did something else besides obsess about journalism.

I spent the most time on the files for the newspaper.

She had several thick files on hate groups. I flipped through them. Most were online newspaper articles she had printed out.

Nothing personal.

"Raya?" I hollered. She came and lifted her coffee mug to her mouth, which instantly steamed her glasses. I gestured toward the empty spot on the desk.

"Did Sasha have a laptop?"

She scrunched her face together. "Yes. It's not there?"

I shook my head.

She bit her lip, thinking. "She didn't take it to the city with her."

"Are you sure?"

"Yes. I met her for coffee near the BART station in Oakland before the protest. She only had on her little cross body bag. Her laptop doesn't fit in that. When she carries her laptop, she has a special bag with padding and stuff."

"Where's her laptop bag?"

Raya went to the side of the desk near the window. "It's usually right here if she's home."

"Any idea where it could be?"

"The only place I could think of is the newspaper office. She might have stopped there on her way to the BART station. It's on the way."

"One more question," I said as I walked toward the door. "Did Sasha keep a journal or diary?"

"I don't know."

Before I walked out, I paused. "Any reason you didn't go with her to the city?" I asked softly. The last thing I wanted to do was make this poor girl feel guilty.

She shot me a look. "No way. No how. Sasha and me have been friends forever, but she sometimes gets all crazy about politics and stuff."

I was about to answer when she interrupted. "I should've told her not to go. I should've stopped her. She was so excited. She said she was going to have a major story. Do you think she's okay? I'm so worried." She tugged at her lip with her teeth. "Is she okay? Where could she be? It doesn't make any sense."

"I'm sure she's okay," I said. It was pathetic how easily the lie came out of my mouth.

———

WALKING under the giant arch onto the Berkeley campus filled me with regret and longing and guilt. Maybe someday I would go back to school. I knew my parents had always planned for me to go to U.C. Berkeley. I'd thought I would, too, but plans changed.

For instance, I hadn't planned on my parent's getting murdered.

Or later, my brother and my godfather's murders.

When my parents died, I enrolled in the San Francisco Art Institute, but didn't even last a semester. I was too interested in numbing my grief with drinking, drugs, and sex. Art school became somewhere for me to meet cute boys. I was asked to leave school after I posed nude when the model didn't show up. It probably didn't help that I slept with the professor, too.

As I walked across campus, past college kids in sweatshirts noses into their phones, my own cell dinged with a text from Dante. Shit! I'd forgotten he and Bobby were coming over for dinner.

"The board is trying to squash Swanson Place. I only now got wind of it."

I texted him back. "Can u help me? Do digging on the board – their bank accounts, etc. Ask Sal for help. They're hiding something. I'm caught up in something else. Fill u in later."

The campus newspaper wasn't the sort of dark and dank gritty spot I'd always imagined a newspaper office to be like. It was underground, sure. But it was brightly lit and modern.

Bookshelves crammed with reference materials lined the walls. Tables scattered across the room held desktop computers or docking stations for laptops and tablets and smart phones. Students typed furiously on keypads or had excited conversations. I stood in the doorway trying to figure out who was in charge. Finally, I saw an older man in jeans, cowboy boots, and a tie. He had longish gray hair swept back from his forehead, a neat beard, and penetrating eyes behind large glasses.

"Excuse me." I approached him. "My name's Gia Santella. I'm a friend of Sasha Fitzgerald's family. Can we go someplace private to talk?"

His smile had faded when I said Sasha's name.

"Sure. Just a second." He turned to a student. "Josh, keep an eye out for Brody's copy. He's ten minutes late. I'll be back in twenty."

He turned to me and stuck out his hand. "I'm Bruce Baumann. My office is across the hall."

11

ANTIFA

THE WALLS OF HIS OFFICE WERE COVERED WITH FRAMED CERTIFICATES and yellowed front pages from newspapers across the country, including one from the New York Times on 9/11. It had a little plaque beside it saying the story had won a Pulitzer. I gestured to it, eyes wide.

"Another life," he said and smiled.

He closed the door and took a seat in one of two worn leather office chairs in front of the desk.

"What have you heard about Sasha?" he asked.

"You know she's missing?"

"Hell yes, I know. She's my star reporter. She didn't file a story from the protest. I called her phone about fifty times. Finally, I went and knocked on the door of her house. Her roommate told me she never came home."

I watched as he spoke. I knew I could trust him.

"Whatever happened to her," I said, "I don't think it's good."

He pressed his lips together tightly, shook his head, and waited for me to continue.

"Is this confidential?" I asked.

He gave me a look. "Consider yourself a source."

I lifted an eyebrow.

"It means I'll go to jail before I reveal my sources." He ran a hand through his hair. "It wouldn't be the first time," he said it so low I barely heard.

I tilted my head. "Okay, then. Somebody saw her dragged away by men in masks. All in black, black masks."

"Antifa!" he said in a low voice and then whistled.

"Who?"

"Stands for Anti-Fascist Action. They are a militant anti-fascist group."

"Oh, yeah. I think I heard of them." I got out a scrap of paper and started taking notes.

"It doesn't make any sense that they would take Sasha," I said. "They oppose hate groups, right?"

"It's a little complicated," he said, "but Antifa stands less for a group and more for a call to action. Anybody can say they are Antifa and get out there with their masks on and basically incite violence."

"Wait? Isn't this the same group that came out to help with Hurricane Harvey relief?"

"Same name. Different people. They're all independent, loosely organized groups using the name and donning the masks. They're known for their masks, and using sticks and clubs to attack others during protests."

I thought about George. They said he'd been clubbed.

"That's one reason Sasha was covering the protest," he said. "Besides her meeting afterward, she was going to interview the members. They claim to protect those who are trying to stand up to the white supremacist groups. And frankly, that probably is true in the rest of the country, but there is a rogue subset here in the Bay Area that we believe is actually run by Kraig King. I told you that each Antifa group is independent? Well, we suspect this local group using the Antifa movement to perpetuate racism."

Kraig King was the national head of the country's largest white supremacist group. He had a home in Berkeley so it made sense he'd be involved in local rallies. But him being behind a group that publicly opposed him? Crazy.

"Like an inside job?"

"Pretty much."

Baumann typed at his laptop and then turned it around to face me. It was an article the student paper had published about possible links between King and Antifa in Berkeley. A giant photo at the top showed a man in a suit standing on a hill overlooking the Oakland protest.

"Whoa." King was the guy who'd stared at me in Katrina's last night. Except in the photo he wore dark sunglasses with his fedora. "Have you ever seen him without the sunglasses and hat?" I asked Baumann.

"Never."

"I saw him with the hat, but without the sunglasses. He was in the Tenderloin the night of the protest."

Baumann paused, thinking. "He was there, huh?"

"You mentioned Sasha was planning to meet someone after the protest? Any idea who she was meeting?" I told him what the blond woman had said, that they took Sasha because she was a reporter.

"She was meeting someone for her story," he said. "Supposed to file that night. She had one more source to check with. It's slated for A1 on Sunday. A blockbuster story. We were going to scoop every paper in the country on this one."

"What's it about?"

He sighed. "I've never given a reporter this sort of leeway before, but Sasha's an exceptional case. She's the best reporter, student or professional, I've worked with in my thirty years in journalism. As far as her story goes, she was keeping it close to the chest. But she did say it involved the mayor's office. Something that would bring the mayor down. In flames."

"Bloody hell!" I flashed back to seeing the mayor coming into Café Katrina's after the protest.

"Yes. Something big."

I was looking at my notes, scribbling and circling words: King. Antifa. Mayor Evans. Protest. Oakland. Berkeley. The Tenderloin.

"Why would King's group have kidnapped Sasha if her story was about the mayor? And why were both of them at Katrina's afterward?"

"Together?" Baumann raised an eyebrow above his glasses.

"No. He left right before Evans and his entourage arrived."

We both sat there in silence, thinking. Finally, I said, "I don't suppose she told you anything about her source?"

"Sasha, like me, protects her sources. She would only tell me if I needed her to and right then I didn't need to know. Now, I'm kicking myself. I should've never let her go off like this, keeping the story to herself. She was just so damn stubborn sometimes. I should've made her tell me everything—for her own good."

"Any idea where she was meeting the source?"

He shook his head.

"But that never happened, did it? They grabbed her at the protest."

"They might have been trying to prevent her from getting to the meeting or maybe her source was behind the kidnapping," he pointed out. "What if he or she was compromised and also grabbed? We don't know much at this point."

I chewed my lip for a minute, thinking. There had to be some clue somewhere as to who her source was. "Her laptop is missing," I said. "Any chance it's somewhere here?"

"I tore the newsroom apart looking for it," he said, opening the door. "But maybe fresh eyes will help. You're welcome to look around. I'll show you where she sits.

As soon as we walked in, a young man rushed up to him.

"Brody just filed. It's in the que." The boy, who had messy hair and blue eyes looked me up and down. He gave me a smirk I think he thought was sexy.

Baumann handed me a card. "My cell is on the back. Call me if you need anything. Josh, can you take Miss Santella over to Sasha's desk? Tell her anything she needs to know."

"Got it."

I scribbled my own number on a scrap of paper and handed it to Baumann before he walked away. "Thank you."

I turned my attention to the boy in front of me who still had that dumb ass look on his face. I drew back and took him in from his pretentious hair down to his Abercrombie tight sweatshirt, shorts and expensive sneakers. I admit, I might have lingered a little on his crotch. Then, I met his eyes and smiled.

Unnerved, a red flush crept up his neck and he turned away. "This way."

In a far corner was a desk below a map of Berkeley. The desktop computer screen was pushed off to the side, along with a keyboard. A few books were stacked in a corner. The desk was covered with a large calendar.

"I'm looking for her laptop," I said, not wasting time on chitchat with Big Man on Campus.

"It's usually right here if she's in the office." He tapped the desk top and then leaned down peering under the desk. "Otherwise, if she's out at class or something, she'll sometimes tuck it into her bag down here."

He stood back up. "Not there."

I sat at her desk.

Josh cleared his throat behind me. "Is Sasha okay?"

His voice made me soften. I turned in the chair. "I don't know. I'm trying to find out. You friends?"

He shrugged. "Yeah."

"Do you have any idea who she was meeting at the protest or where?"

He frowned and looked off in the distance. "She was really excited but she didn't tell me anything. She kept skipping around the newsroom saying the Pulitzer was hers."

I laughed, but then quickly sobered. Turning back to the desk, I grabbed the calendar, going straight to the other night.

It said, "Eddy. 12. KKK."

Standing, I walked out without another word. Walking back to my car, I thought about calling James with what I'd found, but decided to sit on it for now. I'd call him when I had more to report. Meanwhile, I had next to nothing to work with: a partial license plate number and some scribbles on a calendar.

Who was Eddy? Was she meeting him at 12, midnight? Was he a Klu Klux Klan member? Or did it mean something else, altogether?

12

BUILT FOR SPEED

STUCK IN TRAFFIC WAITING TO GET ONTO THE BAY BRIDGE, I CURSED all the people in the Bay Area who apparently had nothing better to do than clog traffic.

I rolled down my windows, letting the breeze from the water wash over me and cranked the Jetset Junkies to drown out the cat calls from the moron in the lane beside me.

Yes, it's a Ferrari. Yes, it's mine, not my daddy's or my baby's daddy's.

My music came to an abrupt halt as my phone chimed through the car speakers.

Bobby.

"Hey." I tried to sound nonchalant, but my voice betrayed me.

"Hey." He cleared his throat. Was he nervous? "We still on for tonight?"

Hearing Bobby's voice always made me a little weak in the knees. No other boy had ever had quite that effect on me. Today was the day Bobby and Dante were going to meet. Dante was making dinner for us and Bobby was going to stay the weekend with me. I'd been both nervous and excited about it for the last week. That is, until Sasha was taken.

For a split second, I considered canceling, but then realized that it was what I always did: run off to be by myself when things got complicated.

"Yes. I'm really looking forward to it, but something's come up."

"Are you canceling?"

"No, I just meant that I have some stuff going on I need to tell you about." I lowered my voice. "I really, really want you to come. But I might be busy this weekend with some other stuff. You can tag along, if you don't mind." I grimaced. I sounded so wimpy, and uncertain.

"What's going on?" he asked, his voice full of concern.

"You have a few minutes?" I asked.

By the time I got to the toll gate, I'd told Bobby the whole story.

"What can I do?" It was the first thing he said when I finished and it made me smile. He was just my speed.

Traffic on the bridge had slowed to a stop and I gazed out over Treasure Island to where my Russian Hill apartment building was. It protruded from the highest hill in the city. I dropped my gaze to the left where the Tenderloin was and where my new home would be soon.

Bobby repeated his offer. "I want to help. Tell me what to do."

"I'm not sure. I need to get in touch with the TV station. They had a helicopter up that night. I need to find that woman with blond hair. I need to find out who Eddy is? I don't even know where to start. I just want you to understand why I might seem a little antsy tonight or distracted."

"You're doing what you can," he said. "You did right to chase after Sasha. You got a plate number. That's huge," his voice was firm. "And you got something at the newspaper. We'll try to figure out what it means. We can call the TV station. And if something comes up tonight, we'll skip dinner and chase that lead. Got it?"

Bobby got me.

"Thank you." I said softly. "See you soon." I clicked off and felt a weight lift off me that I hadn't realized was there. I couldn't cancel on Bobby and Dante, but the thought of drinking and partying with Sasha missing didn't sit well. I couldn't get the look in Darling's eyes out of my mind. The strongest woman I know reduced to a fearful child.

When I got to my place, Dante was already there and something smelled amazing.

I kissed him on the cheek. "You're already cooking?"

"My sous chef was MIA, but I managed to get started."

"It's going to take six hours for you to make dinner?"

"At least." He seemed offended that I would think otherwise. His dark hair was pulled back off his face. So cute.

"Do you always wear a man bun when you cook?"

"Always. Where's Django?"

I ignored his question. I swear everyone cared about that damn dog more than me. I threw out my arms and stretched luxuriously. "I'm so happy you're here."

"Ditto, *paesana*." He looked up and smiled. He looked good. His olive skin glowed and his eyes were bright.

"What's on the menu, Julia Child?"

He rubbed his palms together. This was his favorite part. "Traditional Corsican saffron-infused risotto with scallops, scampi, and ranch quail eggs served with garlic-infused squash blossom fritters followed by a wild fennel, watercress, and rocket salad sprinkled with a rosé vinaigrette. For dessert, a simple but refreshing lingonberry gelato."

I shrieked and ran over to grab him around the waist, twirling him around. "I don't even know what the hell you just said, but I know it's going to be fabulous!" I grabbed his face and kissed his cheeks so many times he grew red.

"You are the maestro!" I drew away and did a deep bow. Then I remembered Sasha and was filled with guilt. I reached for the bourbon, pouring us each at least three fingers.

He raised an eyebrow as I handed the crystal glass to him.

"But seriously, where is Django?"

"My dog is having an extended sleepover at the salon for now. I'll fill you in on what's going on. It's Darling's granddaughter."

By the time I'd finished, we'd both downed the bourbon and poured more.

"Oh, boy."

"Yup." I took a big gulp. "So that's why I couldn't help you with the curmudgeons on the board. Any luck?"

He looked thoughtful. "Maybe. Sal gave me some ideas where to look. I think I might have stumbled onto something."

I raised my glass to him. "You've always been my favorite partner in crime, Dante." I was starting to feel buzzed from the booze and it made me sentimental.

"Well, it sounds like there's a replacement waiting in the wings."

I raised an eyebrow and he smiled. "I can't wait to meet him."

My stomach erupted in nervous flutters.

"I'm worried sick about Sasha, but I am going to try to set that aside and enjoy the two most important men in my life meeting for the first time."

I poured us glasses of red wine from the bottle I had opened the night before. "*Salut!*"

"What? You trying to get us drunk before he even gets here."

"Drink!"

"*Salut!*" he said and took a small sip. "Oh, Gia. You have fine taste in wine. Awful taste in clothes and men, but fine taste in wine."

I gave him a playful punch in the arm. "Stop. I told you that Bobby was different."

He winked. "He must be different because he's the first boy you've ever introduced me to."

"Really?" I was surprised to hear it, but when I thought back I realized he was right. Dante was too special for anyone else to meet. My stomach tumbled. I only hoped they would like each other. Otherwise, I'd be devastated. They *had* to like each other, didn't they?

While Dante was busy in the kitchen, I sneaked into my bedroom to make a few calls. If I didn't do at least something to try to find Sasha tonight, my anxiety would ruin everything.

I called Channel 5 first. The friendly receptionist told me my best bet was to come by the studio in the morning. The same crew who covered the protest would be working then. I should ask for the producer. Then I called James and left a message asking him to call me if he had any luck tracing the license plate. My last call was to Darling. The salon manager, Shelley, told me that Darling was sleeping. That she hadn't slept at all the night before and now had finally crashed. I didn't want to wake her so I told Shelley I'd be by in the morning.

———

THE CANDLES WERE LIT and the lights dimmed. Bobby would be here soon. I was nervous, so I let off steam by dancing around to the White Stripe's "Seven Nation Army" while singing at the top of my lungs. I kept annoying Dante trying to get him to dance with me. He finally banished me to the living room.

"Did I mention you have awful taste in music, too?" Dante hollered from the kitchen.

"Oh, be quiet, you old fart. This is what all the hip kids are listening to."

"Using the word 'hip' makes you unhip," he yelled back. I hid my smile in case he was looking.

The entire apartment smelled amazing from Dante's magic in my kitchen.

Until Bobby arrived I would dance. As night fell, my giant windows reflected my shadowy figure moving around like a banshee. I never bothered to close my blackout shades. I didn't give a damn if someone wanted to watch me walk around naked or dance like a madwoman. It wasn't worth the claustrophobic feeling I'd get closing off my views. However, the contractor was installing smart windows in my new place in the Tenderloin. My phone would allow me to control the tint on the solar-powered windows to dim the sunlight in my eyes or provide complete privacy.

Until I moved, I'd live the way I always did: transparently.

My building was the tallest one in the city so anyone spying would have to be some pervert in a nearby building. Besides, the stupendous views were why I bought the place. To the north was a view of Fisherman's Wharf and Alcatraz. Off to the left—the Golden Gate Bridge. To the west was North Beach—the Italian section of town—then beyond that Treasure Island and to the right of that—a smidge of the Bay Bridge.

"Gia, can you come here, a sec?"

I turned off the music and headed into the kitchen. He was stirring something that smelled like heaven.

"I'm glad to see you getting involved in this Swanson Place."

"Yeah." I instantly felt uncomfortable.

"But once that's over, what do you think you want to do?"

I took a slug of wine and shrugged. "What do you mean? I'll do what I always do." Nothing. Drink. Smoke pot. Have sex. Do karate.

He frowned. "Gia. You need to do something. Being involved in your dad's company could be a really great thing for you. You're a brilliant woman doing nothing with your mind."

"I'm doing something."

He raised an eyebrow.

"I'm helping find Darling's granddaughter." It sounded lame even to me.

"Gia." His tone said it all.

"I haven't decided what to do with my life, yet." I was whining. It was not attractive, I knew.

I swallowed the dismay rising in my throat and looked away.

"Swanson Place is a great project for you. It speaks to your passion to help people. I think you really could do a lot with projects like that."

Without answering, I grabbed the bottle of bourbon and left the kitchen. I stepped out on the balcony to sneak a cigarette.

Making Swanson Place happen would be really good for me. But was it as altruistic as it appeared or was it truly selfish? Something for me to ease my enormous crushing guilt over Ethel's death. I'd asked her to get a message to Kato and not long after that she'd ended up dead. I'd thrown this innocent woman with nothing more than the clothing on her back to the wolves. The Sicilian Mafia was after me and she got in the way. She was no match.

They disposed of her without a second thought.

I couldn't prove it, but the coincidences were too staggering.

They killed my mother, father, brother, and godfather. They tried to kill Kato, but were interrupted. Why wouldn't they kill a poor homeless woman who stood in their way?

But Ethel, like Kato, should never have been brought into their sights. That was on me.

Pushing all those thoughts back, I decided I was going to try to enjoy this night of good food, yummy wine, and amazing company. I'd done everything I could tonight to find Sasha. Maybe I'd have better luck in the morning.

As I thought this, the doorbell rang and my pulse raced.

I hadn't seen Bobby in two weeks. Two long weeks.

Quickly, I stubbed my cigarette out in my L' Hotel Paris ashtray and sprayed my tongue with some of the mint mist I kept on the balcony.

I FLUFFED my hair and fixed my lipstick in front of the giant and ridiculously expensive Waterford Crystal mirror hanging on the wall inside my front door. Dante grinned over my shoulder.

"You're acting like a school girl going to prom for the first time."

I swatted him. "You know I never went to prom."

"Not my fault."

"Was, too. You're the one who had to get a compound fracture skateboarding two days before prom."

"You could've gone with a million other guys. I have no idea why you wanted to go with your gay best friend."

"I didn't want to go with anyone else."

I watched in the mirror as a flush appeared on my cheeks. We both knew it was because I was in love with Dante at the time and refused to believe that I couldn't change his mind.

Dante, who read my mind as he always did, leaned over and kissed my cheek.

"It's way better this way. We will be friends forever. We are *famiglia*, Gia. Nothing will ever change that. I love you."

"I love you, too, Dante."

Luckily a knock on the door broke through the sentimental moment. I took a deep breath, smoothed down my skirt, and opened the door. For a second, I froze, staring at Bobby. He wore a white shirt unbuttoned a little to reveal his smooth, tanned, hairless chest, faded jeans and flip flops. Totally beach boy in the big city. I took him in and smiled. To some people, he probably looked like an average attractive guy. But when he smiled at me—he flat out took my breath away.

He was smiling now.

"Can I come in?"

I was startled out of my lust-filled stupor. Even after several months of dating he still did that to me. When he kissed me, I was intoxicated by the smell of his skin and the taste of his mouth. I didn't want it to end, but could feel Dante's presence over my shoulder. I drew back and clapped my hands together.

"Bobby Kostas, I'd like you to meet my dearest friend, my brother, really, Dante Marino." I gestured toward Dante. "Dante, this is ... Bobby."

The two shook hands heartily and smiled and then Bobby grabbed Dante and brought him in for a hug. And no, there is no goddamn way those were tears. Must've been the onions.

13

ORGASMIC

Bobby speared his first bite and then closed his eyes as he chewed. I waited and watched, shooting an amused look at Dante, who held his finger to his lips.

When Bobby opened his eyes, he shook his head. "Hot damn." His smile lit up his face.

"It's orgasmic, isn't it?"

"I have no words," Bobby said.

"It defies description, right?"

"Exactly."

"You two are too kind," Dante said with false modesty. "But, really, thank you. I truly appreciate it."

I couldn't stop grinning. "I always love it when someone tries Dante's cooking for the first time."

"I can see why. It's life changing," Bobby said, taking a sip of his wine.

Over his shoulder, I could see my reflection in the mirrored dining room wall. The candle light was flattering. My eyes were sparkling and my cheeks pink. My dark hair was mussed a little bit from me running my hands through it.

That, I told myself, *is the face of a happy woman.*

But then Sasha's face came back to me. How could I sit here enjoying myself when she could be hurt or dead somewhere? I remembered Darling grabbing my hand and making me promise to find her granddaughter. Shit.

If only I had got the name or number of that woman who had seen the kidnapping. She might have information that could help me track down the kidnappers. If only I knew what the words on Sasha's calendar meant. I closed my eyes. I was a failure. I sat here drinking and laughing and Sasha could be dead somewhere.

But here I was.

Suddenly, my appetite was gone. Too many bad thoughts and feelings were surfacing. Things I kept pressed down deep inside. My own mother loved my brother more than me. I was unlovable. And a fuck up.

I reached over and poured more wine into my glass, downing it and then poured some more. Dante raised an eyebrow at me that I ignored.

Bobby pretended not to notice. His first mistake. "When are we going to take a weekend trip up to Calistoga?" he said.

A wave of unease passed through me. What the hell was wrong with me? Bobby's affections suddenly felt suffocating and I didn't know why. I didn't want to spend a weekend with him. I didn't even know if I wanted to spend the rest of this night with him.

A pall had fallen over the table.

"I'll get more wine." I stood. Behind me in the mirror, I saw Bobby shoot Dante a look. Dante shrugged.

I was a disaster. Cursed. The dysfunction was rearing its ugly head. I'd thought I could keep it at bay. Boy, was I wrong. In an instant, I'd changed the whole tenor of our lovely dinner party. I was an asshole. I sucked.

Bobby and Dante struck up a conversation about the San Francisco Forty-Niners. Probably to cover up the awkwardness I'd created. Making sure they weren't looking, I poured a good-sized slug of bourbon in my glass, downed it, poured another, downed it, and then grabbed a bottle of red from my counter.

The booze hit me like a Mac truck. I stumbled a little as I entered the small dining room's space. Dante shot me a concerned look over Bobby's head. I rolled my eyes at him. I could handle myself. I was fine. If anyone could handle their booze, it was this girl. I had drunk bigger men under the table more times than I could count. I poured another glass of wine and smiled, trying to ease the tension.

"To the two most handsome, talented men in San Francisco!" I lifted my glass. Sure, my words might have been a teeny tiny bit slurred. It was all good. I could get smashed in my own place to celebrate this momentous moment. I didn't have to drive. I was already home. I was with two people I trusted with my life. It was all good.

How much trouble could I get in?

———

I WAS SLUMPED on the couch with my feet up on the coffee table swirling the ice in my glass.

Dante had just left. Bobby was beside me looking down. His forehead was furrowed. He reached for my glass.

"Maybe we should get you started on some water."

I straightened up. "Yeah. I don't want a hangover tomorrow." I set my glass down and gratefully took the big glass of water Bobby handed me. "Thanks."

I gulped most of it and then felt a little sick. The flicker of the dying candles made stationary objects appear to shift and undulate.

"I don't think I should be here enjoying myself, right now."

Bobby traced his fingertips on my bare arm, sending shivers and waves of desire through me. "Is that what's been bothering you tonight?"

"Yeah," I admitted. "I am selfish."

"You are not selfish. You have the biggest heart out of anyone I've ever met."

I gave him a doubtful look. He must be drunk, too.

"Is there anything you could be doing right now to find her?"

I thought about it. "I guess not."

"Then, quit thinking about it. I'll help you get your mind on other things."

He leaned over and within seconds we were both naked, our clothes flung across the room and I was astride him on the couch, giving any neighborhood perverts the show of their life.

Later, after we had moved to the bedroom for round two and had taken a long shower together afterward, I heard Bobby clear his throat.

I felt a wave of apprehension trickle through me.

"Gia," he propped himself up on one elbow and looked over at me in the candlelight.

"Yes?" I could hear the nervousness in my voice. Was he dumping me?

"I was thinking. We've been dating for six months now, right?"

I nodded, too nervous to speak.

"And I'm moving up here in January, right?"

"Uh huh."

"What would you think," he looked down and ran his fingers across my bare belly. "What would you think about making this something ..."

He broke off and I watched him swallow. He was nervous. It made my mouth go dry.

"What do you think about being exclusive?"

I closed my eyes.

"That bad, huh?" He said. He sat up and I could hear a flicker of both anger and hurt in his voice. His hand left my belly.

I opened my eyes and took a deep breath. "I'm not ... I'm just not sure."

"Fine." He crossed his arms and looked away.

"I told you when I get close to someone ..."

He waved his hand angrily. "Yes, you run away. I know that. Somehow I was stupid enough to think that I was different than all those other guys you 'get close to and run away from.'"

I sat up now. "But you are!"

Now he stood. "And yet, you are lumping me in right with them and reacting the same way."

"It's different." I love *you.*

He narrowed his eyes at me. "And how's that?"

"I don't know." Because I suck.

"Great." He stood and hunted around on the floor. He grabbed his T-shirt and yanked it on.

"Are you leaving?" My voice was nearly a shriek.

"Why should I stay?"

I took a deep breath. "It's different because with you, I'm scared."

"Oh, that makes me feel a lot better," he said sarcastically and tugged on his jeans.

"I'm terrified." Please don't make me say it. Please.

"Even better." He yanked his phone from my charger and headed for the doorway of my bedroom.

"Gia, when you figure out whether or not you're ready to have a relationship with me—on my terms, which means only dating me—give me a call."

"Bobby!" I yelled it. "I swear I'm not sleeping with anyone else. That's not what this is about."

He looked at me for a long moment. "That's what being exclusive means." He waited, staring. I wanted, more than anything, to rush over and kiss him and tell him I'd commit to him and would be exclusive but something deep inside me stopped me from moving. I was frozen, paralyzed. I couldn't speak a word.

After a few seconds, he sighed and left, slamming the front door behind him.

Deja vu. Flashbacks of James storming off came into focus. He didn't say the same words, but it's exactly why he walked away, as well. I was fucked up, totally incapable of having a relationship.

I lay in bed until the candles completely burned out.

Around four in the morning, I threw back the covers and got dressed. Pulling the collar of my leather jacket up, I laced up my motorcycle boots, tucked my gun in its holster, grabbed a fifth of Wild Turkey and headed toward the Tenderloin.

The night was dank and cold and anyone with half a brain was already tucked in bed or bundled up in blankets in an alley. Once I was at the plaza, I stood staring at the place where George had lain on the ground. Then, imagining a group in masks grabbing Sasha, I headed toward the spot where I'd seen them stuff Sasha in the SUV, hoping that somehow just by being there and retracing her abduction, I would have a clue where she was.

I stood and took a slug of the whiskey as I stared at the spot where I'd last seen Sasha.

After a few minutes I sat down, putting my back against a small wall. In the orange glow of the streetlights I spotted a shadowy bulk moving closer. If I squinted, instead of a man pushing an overflowing shopping cart, it looked like a hulking, lumbering Grizzly bear headed my way.

When the man was a few feet away, I recognized him.

"Why aren't you sleeping, Sly?"

He shook his head. "Charlie coming to get me when I close my eyes. If I go to sleep, I'm dead man walking."

"Oh honey, you're safe now." I patted his back. "The war's been over a long time, my friend."

"The V.C. never sleeps." He sighed. "I gotta be on guard."

I had nothing to say to that. The Viet Cong weren't in San Francisco, but there was somebody out there making people disappear.

Standing up, I brushed off my jeans and handed him the whiskey. He took a gulp and handed the bottle back to me.

I shook my head. "All yours. Stay safe out there."

14

LOIS LANE

THE NEXT MORNING, I WOKE UP FURIOUS FOR SLEEPING SO LATE. IT WAS ten. I hadn't gone to bed until six, but still. I had a shit ton to do. I was also angry with Bobby. He gave up on me so easily. It was his fault for bringing up getting exclusive and shit.

I didn't understand what was wrong with the way our relationship had been going. Why had he tried to rush things? It didn't even make sense. If he was already living in San Francisco, then I could understand him wanting to be exclusive, but hell, we were still in a long-distance relationship. There was no need to get excited and put labels on it.

If he was serious about me, he would wait and not push it.

He had ruined everything. I repeated this story to myself all morning as I drank my coffee, showered, and put on makeup. But deep down, I knew it was a story I was telling myself to feel better.

On top of it all I was exhausted and slightly hung over. My head throbbed with a headache. During the few hours I slept, I'd tossed and turned with nightmares. They all involved me searching for Sasha or trying to find that blond-haired woman or the masked men in the SUV. Each time I thought I was close, when I spotted Sasha or the vehicle, something would get between us: A train. A wall. A body of water.

———

The receptionist at Channel 5 instantly shot me down.

"Without an appointment, I'm sorry I can't let you back there." She was a woman probably in her forties with a blond bob who looked twenty from behind and eighty from the front. She had circles of wrinkles around her mouth from smoking. Even from across the desk I could smell the stench of cigarette smoke emanating from her clothing.

Another good reason to kick the cancer sticks.

"Didn't I talk to you yesterday?" I was confused.

"No."

"The woman I spoke to yesterday told me to come by today and ask for the producer. Can you at least call the producer?"

"I'm sorry, no."

"Can you give me the name of the producer?"

"I'm sorry."

"You can't or you won't?"

"I'm sorry. It's Saturday. We have a skeleton staff. I'm sure they're too busy to talk to you. You're going to have to call and make an appointment." She pushed a tiny rack of business cards toward me.

"How do I know who to ask for? Who to make the appointment with?"

"You can call and ask for the producer's name."

I stared at her, dumbfounded.

The ability to quickly overcome seemingly insurmountable roadblocks and obstacles that the enemy places in the way is the sign of a true warrior. If you can't go over the mountain, go under it or around it.

I tilted my head. "Hold on. So, you're telling me if I call I'll get all the information I need?"

"You can call and learn who they are and then you can be

connected to them and ask for an appointment. That is the way things are done here. Especially on the weekends."

I grabbed a card and took out my cell phone. I punched in the number and then stared at her. The phone in front of her rang. I could see her swallow. Then it rang again. She studiously ignored it.

I held my phone away from my mouth. "Your phone is ringing."

Acting like she'd been told to lick poop, the woman reached out and picked up the phone. "Channel 5."

"Hi, how are you today?"

She rolled her eyes.

"I was wondering if you could tell me the name of a producer in the newsroom and connect me so I can make an appointment."

"One moment please."

She pressed hold and without looking at me, dialed another number.

"It's Bridgette. I have someone on the line who wants a producer in breaking news. Is Al available?"

Al. At least I got a first name. I rolled my eyes as she waited, listening to the voice on the other end. *I can play along with this fucking charade as long as you want, lady.*

Bridgette got a smug look on her face and then hung up. I heard her voice on my line now. "I'm sorry," she said, looking at me with triumph. "Nobody is available to take your call right now. You— "

I hung up and walked out. Time to go around the mountain.

I stood in front of the building, looking up at the mirrored windows. The building was surrounded on three sides by a gated parking lot. There had to be a back door, someplace employees could take a smoke break or something. The woman on the phone yesterday said the same crew who filmed the protest was working today. I needed a plan to get through Bridgette the Guard Dog.

That's when I saw a Channel 5 news van at the stoplight waiting to turn into a gate leading into the parking lot. I dashed over and flung myself in front of the van right before it got to the gate. The driver slammed on the brakes. I put my palm on the warm hood and smiled.

I came over to the driver's side window. "Sorry about the dramatics."

"What the hell is your problem?" The driver had 1970s sideburns and wore jeans that looked like they'd been worn nonstop since that same era.

"I need some help," I said, leaning into his window. "The pit bull at reception told me to take a hike. All I want is to talk to someone who covered the protest. I heard the same crew was working today. Is that you?"

He scowled. "Bridgette is such a pain."

"Understatement. Are you going to help me or not?" Was the dude hard of hearing?

"Hop in."

I raised an eyebrow but didn't waste any time rushing over to the passenger door and jumping in. The gate opened and we pulled into the employee lot. I didn't say a word, afraid to jinx my luck. He backed up into a spot in the shade against the building and undid his seatbelt.

"I was up in the chopper. I got some footage." He turned to me with a look. "Why you asking? What's your angle?"

I stopped myself from rolling my eyes. "My angle is my friend was dragged out of the plaza by masked men—maybe Antifa—and hasn't been seen since."

"If I show you the footage, what's in it for me?"

"The scoop of your life."

He yawned, nonplussed.

"After the paper prints it, you can go live. I'll make sure you're the only station with the story for at least the first part of the day."

"What's the story, Lois Lane?"

"I can't tell you yet, but the girl who was taken is a journalist. And they kidnapped her to stop her from printing it."

He opened his door. "Come on. Let's get in the back and I'll show you what I got from that night."

In the back, I watched footage of the protest from the sky. Unfortunately, much of it was from a bird's eye perspective. Every once in a while, the camera zoomed in on some smaller skirmishes on the ground. After nearly twenty minutes, I saw something in the area where I believed Sasha had been.

"Can you pause or zoom in here?"

"I can't zoom, but I can pause."

I got as close as I could to the still image on the screen. It sure as hell looked like a small pink dot surrounded by figures in black. "Okay, can you run it slow motion?"

I watched as the pink dot and the black figures moved off the screen and toward the edge of the protest.

It was the moment Sasha was kidnapped.

"There it is!" I leaned forward.

When she got to the edge of the screen she disappeared. He paused it there.

I stared at the screen, reluctant to give up that easily. I'd hoped for a lot more.

The cameraman moved to turn off the video.

"Wait!" I nearly jumped out of my seat. I pointed at the corner of the screen. "What is that?"

He leaned in and narrowed his eyes. "It's a drone. It kept getting in my way and buzzing us."

"Buzzing us?"

"Haven't you seen Top Gun? When Tom Cruise buzzed the air traffic control tower?"

I frowned.

He sighed. "It's a term that means he was being annoying, like a fly, and got super close to us and our blades. Once he even got right in front of my camera."

"Where's that footage?"

He leaned forward and hit play. "Any second I imagine."

After a minute or two the drone appeared right in front of the camera.

"Bastard," the cameraman said.

"Any idea where it came from? Who's operating it?"

He chuckled. "I was so pissed I actually had the pilot swoop and try to take it out and the little fucker went and hid in an apartment. Watch."

For a few minutes the camera filmed the crowd of protesters below dispersing and then zoomed in on the drone. There was a jerky motion as the helicopter swooped down and the drone took off. The camera zoomed in on a building two blocks away where the drone zipped into a window.

"Can you pause it right here?"

A shadowy figure appeared in the window. It was too far away to distinguish any features or gender.

"Now can you play in slow mo?"

The drone entered the window, the figure disappeared and was replaced by a black shade. When the camera zoomed out again I asked him to pause it one more time.

The window was ten up from the ground and two over from the right side. The red brick building was on the corner two blocks away from the plaza in the Whoa-Man neighborhood of the Tenderloin.

I scribbled my number on another scrap of paper and handed it to the guy.

"What's your name?"

"Jimmy."

"Got a card?"

"Nah, I'm just a photog." He leaned over and ripped a piece of notebook paper out. "Here's my number. I'll be waiting for that scoop."

I looked him right in the eye. "You can count on it." I meant it, too.

He pointed toward a gate in the fence. "You can get out that way."

15

THE DARK NET

MY FERRARI WOULD PROBABLY BE FIREBOMBED IF I PARKED IT IN THE Tenderloin. At the very least, it would get a few key scratches along its sides, so I decided to go home, park it in the garage and grab some food upstairs before I headed to the building in the Tenderloin. My car was my baby and I wanted to keep it nice as long as I could. My last Ferrari had ended up a heaping pile of twisted metal at the bottom of a Marin cliff. My doorman had made the fatal decision to take it joyriding right after someone cut the brake line.

Upstairs at my place, last night's argument with Bobby came back full force as I stared at a cold plate of leftovers. It had started out as the best night ever, and then, as was typical in my life, ended in a massive pile of shit.

I chewed a few bites of the food that had suddenly become taste-less before I pushed the plate away. Instead, I poured a shot of bourbon and went out on the balcony where my smokes were stashed. It was past noon. I glanced at the clock. Barely past noon.

I had thirty hours until James went to his supervisor.

I had brought the bottle of bourbon with me onto the balcony so I poured another shot and smoked a cigarette. I thought of the pit bull receptionist's heavily-lined mouth and stubbed out my second cigarette halfway through.

When I stood, I had a little bit of a buzz. I eyed the bottle but decided I needed to be halfway sober to confront the drone operator. The bottle had a magnetic pull. It would help me tamp down the ugliness I felt inside about Bobby leaving.

But then I snapped out of it.

I had no time—and no right—to feel sorry for myself. I had everything money could buy and good health to boot and here I was having a fucking pity party. Look at Ethel: never had a damn good thing in her life and now she's dead in the ground. I had no right to wallow in self-pity. No wonder Bobby stormed out. I didn't blame him. I would've done the same exact thing.

I would find Sasha and make everything all right.

On my way out the door, I decided my first stop in the Tenderloin should be Darling's salon. I needed to tell her what I'd learned at the campus newspaper and ask her about Eddy and KKK and 12. Then I would try to find the person who operated that drone and see if they had any camera footage that would help me find Sasha. I squared my shoulders and grabbed my bag.

I could have my very own pity party later—after I brought Sasha home safe.

———

FOR ONCE, instead of people jeering at me asking why a white girl was in the salon, everyone was hushed when I walked in. A few women in their chairs raised their eyebrows and shot looks at one another when they saw me. I went straight to Shelley's chair. "What's going on?"

She leaned over and said in a low voice. "Miss Darling won't let anyone in back there. We're all worried about her."

"Oh no." I rushed right to the back door and knocked firmly.

"Darling? Open up."

Nothing.

Fear spiked through me. "Darling? I've got to talk to you." I looked up at the camera pointing down at me.

Still the door remained closed.

"It's about Sasha goddamn it. Open up." I glanced over my shoulder and saw everyone was staring at me. The door clicked open.

Darling was slumped on the couch in the corner. Django, who'd never been allowed on the furniture before, was curled up beside her. He gave me a guilty look. But I was too concerned about Darling.

I barely recognized her. The put-together, well-dressed and coiffed woman I knew had disappeared. Instead, a woman I barely recognized wearing some stained T-shirt and baggy sweatpants sat there eating twisted crackers covered in neon orange cheese that had stained all ten of her fingers. Her head was bald. I'd never known her elaborate hairstyles were wigs. Dark bags cupped her eyes, which were red from crying.

I rushed over and crawled onto the couch to hug her. Django turned his head away from me. He thought he was in trouble for being on the couch.

"Darling, pull yourself together. We're going to find her. I've got some leads. I just wanted to stop and check in on you for a minute. Make sure you're taking care of yourself so I don't have to sit here with you and I can be out there finding Sasha."

I was guilt tripping her into pulling it together.

Just then my phone rang. I didn't recognize the number, but couldn't afford not to answer it. Not if it was someone who might know something about Sasha.

"Gia." I answered, eying Darling, who was absentmindedly patting Django and wiping her nose with tissues.

"It's Bruce Baumann, from the paper."

"Hey."

"I thought you should know that I got an email from the dark net saying that if Sasha's story was printed, we would never see her again."

"Okay." I kept my voice neutral. Darling raised an eyebrow, suspecting something.

"Can I call you back in a few minutes?"

"Sure."

"By the way, what's the dark net?"

"It's an encrypted part of the Internet. Where nothing can be traced. Where everything nefarious happens."

"Um, can you be more specific?"

"It's an underground network where you can buy anything you ever imagined. WikiLeaks is on the dark web."

"Gotcha." I said. "I'll call you back in a few."

I hung up and turned toward Darling. "Did Sasha ever mention anyone named Eddy?"

Darling shook her head.

"Okay. Call me if you remember anything else. I have to go, but I'm not going to let you sit here by yourself and deal with this alone. Who can I call to come be with you? Who do you trust?"

She sniffled. "I'm fine."

"I said I'm not going to let you sit here alone. Who? Now." My voice was firm. I knew it was the only thing Darling would respond to.

"I'm not alone. I got my new dog keep me company." She gave me a look.

"My dog."

"Whatev," she waved me off with her hand.

"Darling, call someone right now to come be with you until we find Sasha." I hoped she couldn't read my mind because what I was really thinking was I wanted someone to be with her if what I found out wasn't good.

Sighing, she reached for her phone. "I'll call my sister Precious. She'll come."

"Promise?"

Darling nodded. I gestured at the secret back door out of the office.

"I'm heading out now. Keep your phone by your side. I'll call as soon as I learn something solid. Keep your head up. Stay strong for Sasha."

She gave me a look that told me she didn't need anyone—especially me—telling her to stay strong.

As soon as I'd made it through the maze of stairways and tunnels from Darling's secret exit and emerged a few blocks over, I dialed Baumann.

"Is there any way to trace that message? Any way at all?"

"I really don't think so."

"Can you respond to it?"

"No. I can't even reply."

"Bloody hell."

I hung up and dialed James.

"Any luck on the plate?"

"Still working it. Do you know how many black SUV's there are with license plates that start with 6L? I've got a list from the state DMV I'm narrowing down to those registered in the Bay Area."

"I found out Sasha was working on a story exposing the mayor."

"Exposing the mayor to what?"

"Hell, if I know? Something big, though."

"That's speculation."

"Jesus, James, this isn't a court of law. I got it from a good source."

Silence.

Anger flared through me. He dismissed what I said like it was nothing. Maybe he shouldn't be a detective after all. I had planned on telling him the detail on Sasha's calendar mentioning an Eddy but decided against it. If he was going to be a dick about it, I wouldn't tell him anything. Besides, for now, the numbers and letters meant nothing. I'd tell him once I figured out what they stood for.

"Okay, then ..." I trailed off waiting for him to say something.

"Six p.m. tomorrow."

I hung up without answering.

16

WHOA-MAN

THE RED-BRICKED BUILDING HAD AN AURA OF NEGLECT. A LOT OF THE buildings in the mostly residential Whoa-Man neighborhood did. Almost all the windows were covered with sheets or blankets instead of curtains. The front door leading into a small lobby had two double dead bolts on it. There were no doorbells to be found. I peered inside a window by the door. A bank of mail boxes lined one wall and a staircase the other.

No elevator in sight. I backed up and looked at the window where the drone had come from. Then I circled the building. There was a fire escape in the alley. Only about ten feet off the ground. The city of San Francisco didn't mess around with fire escapes after the 1906 fire. Most of the Tenderloin had burned to the ground. The buildings around here were all built after the fire.

But the fire escape also signified a way for someone to get to me. A danger, as well, as a safety feature. A double-edged sword. If I were a prospective tenant for this building, I would've immediately been concerned that someone could get up the fire escape and into my building. It wasn't an idle worry. It was exactly what I was going to do.

The alley was full of overflowing trash cans and Dumpsters. The closest Dumpster had wheels. Perfect. I peeked inside. It was empty.

Trash pick-up must've been this morning. I got on one side of it and pushed with my entire body. It moved. I pushed it until it was right underneath the fire escape. Then I closed the lid gently so it wouldn't make a loud bang and pulled myself on top. If I stood on tiptoe, I could reach the small railing that surrounded the platform at the bottom of the fire escape. I clung to the rails and thanked Kato for making me start a push-up and pull-up regime over the past year.

Grunting and groaning, I pulled myself up but my feet lost traction and I slipped back to the top of the Dumpster. I could reach the platform but it was surrounded by a railing. I couldn't get enough of a grip to pull myself over the railing.

You can do it, Gia.

I heard my father's voice in my head. Every time I'd attempted a physical feat just a little beyond my ability, he had urged me on. *You can do it, Giada! You are a Santella.*

A sob caught in my throat. Not very long ago, I'd doubted that. I'd worried that a sadistic murderer was actually the one whose DNA I carried. Luckily, it wasn't true.

I was a Santella through and through. I stepped back and examined the fire escape and the building. There was a slight architectural groove on the building where a brick stuck out. If I pulled myself up, managed to get a foot onto the brick, and gave myself a boost, I could potentially pull myself up and over the railing.

I gave a huge grunt, hoisted myself up to my chest and found a foothold on the brick. But then I slipped.

One more time.

This time, the toe of my motorcycle boot gripped the brick and I was able to pull myself up so my stomach was at the edge of the small railing around the platform. From there, I tumbled over the railing onto the platform.

And just in time. I heard voices below and scooted back against the brick wall, holding my breath. When the voices passed, I began to climb. The first window showed a hallway. Good. All the entrances would be to the hallway and not into people's apartments. I climbed cautiously, peeking into the bottom of each window before I clambered past it.

When I reached the tenth floor, I tried the window. Too easy. It was unlocked. I opened it and listened. It was silent. I ducked inside, leaving the window open behind me in case I needed a quick escape. I was turned around, so it took me a few minutes to figure out which doorway would lead to the drone operator's apartment I'd seen from below. I counted the doorways. Then I figured it out. 10 D.

Before knocking, I pressed my ear to the door and heard a TV. I rapped on the door with my ear still against it. There was no peephole. The TV suddenly went quiet. I rapped again and listened. This time I heard movement.

"Who's there?"

"Gia."

Silence. I backed up.

Then the door cracked. I saw a huge face. Like the biggest face I'd ever seen on a person. The boy or man, or whatever he was, also had long red hair with floppy bangs. He towered over me and peered through the two-inch gap the chain allowed.

"I don't know you," he said in a matter-of-fact voice.

"Yeah. I know. I need your help."

He frowned. "Why me?"

His bulk took up the entire space where the door had opened but I made an educated guess. "I need your expertise. Your tech savvy. You know, your technological know-how."

He scrunched up his face, taking all that in.

"You gonna let me in?" I said with a scowl. "I doubt I'm any threat, right?"

Maybe he realized he was acting like a wuss because he undid the chain opening the door. But still hesitated.

"I don't know. Who are you?"

He drew back as I took a step into his place. The solid weight of my gun in the holster on my back reassured me. I slid past him, patting his chest. "I told you, I'm Gia."

He was a big boy. Enormous. He wore jeans and a flannel shirt over a faded Green Day T-shirt.

"I saw them in Vegas. 2012," I said, nodding at his shirt. "You know the show where Billie Joe Armstrong lost his shit."

His eyes widened. "You saw that show?"

"Hell, yeah, I did."

His arms circled as if he were playing guitar and his voice rose and took on an English accent. "You're giving me one minute? You're fucking kidding me. I'm not Justin Bieber, you fucks!" Then he mimicked smashing his guitar.

"Yeah, that show. Did you know he's from California, even though he sings with a British accent?"

I didn't think his eyes could get any wider. I'd blown his mind, apparently. With the ice now broken, I strode past his ratty couch to the window. "Right here. This is where you fly her, isn't it? Will you show me?"

I turned and smiled. He seemed confused. Out of the corner of my eye, I spotted a huge desk that held three keyboards attached to three giant computer screens.

"Listen, sailor. I got a problem I need your help with. My friend was kidnapped from the protest and I know your drone recorded it. If you can show me that footage, I will make it worth your while." I dug a hundred dollar bill out of my front jeans pocket. "Here's something to start—for your trouble, for letting me in." I threw the bill on the coffee table. "We have a deal?"

He grunted but sat down at a keyboard in front of the bank of computers. "What was the actual date of the protest." Hook, line, and motherfucking sinker.

"No clue. It was two days ago."

He rolled his eyes and flipped a big calendar. Then he scrolled through elaborately timed and dated files that appeared on all three screens. I decided right then that he'd be a good person to be friends with once I moved back into the Tenderloin. He probably had recorded every resident in the neighborhood at some point. Good intel.

Then he clicked on one of the files and video of the protest appeared. It was much closer than the Channel 5 news footage. I could even see Sasha in her pink sweatshirt during one pass. She was on her phone. She looked confused. Then it swung over to another group in the crowd.

"Brilliant! This is good stuff." I crouched beside him with admiration. "How long you been doing this?"

He shrugged. After a few seconds, I asked if he could slow it down.

"Okay, can you fast forward a little." I saw some people in black with masks in the middle of the screen. "Stop!"

I leaned in. They all wore black hooded sweatshirts, black bandannas over their mouth and nose and dark sunglasses. The bandannas and shirts had the words, "Bay Area Antifa" in white.

"That's them." We watched as they confronted another group. I could see Sasha's pink sweatshirt in the corner of the screen. Any minute the Antifa group would grab her. But then, the Antifa group took off in another direction off the screen.

That's when I saw them, a group that was not part of the protest crowd flitted out of the shadows nearby and surrounded Sasha. This group of six wore black clothes and wore black masks. They grabbed Sasha and yanked her off her feet. She tried to fight back but one of them held something to her mouth. She slumped but wasn't knocked out. Her eyes were blinking. They picked her up and carried her away, her feet dragging.

"Pause!"

I studied the masked people. There were six of them. I looked for signs of gender. I didn't see any breasts. They wore black jeans, not tight. Black boots. Black long-sleeve T-shirts and masks. I counted heads. Four of the six had blond hair. The other two had light brown hair. All short military-style cuts. I was fairly certain they were all men.

Unfortunately, there was nothing that would identify them in any way except the two having a different hair color.

"Can you play it again?"

The guy clicked the mouse.

The drone followed the group until they left the plaza.

I turned and he paused the video.

"You knew exactly what I was talking about when I walked in, didn't you? You knew this was fucked up?"

He gave me a look that basically said, "no, duh."

I gave him an appraising look and smiled. "How far did you follow them?"

"Long enough to see you."

He pressed play.

The group made their way to the edge of the plaza and stood waiting. The SUV wasn't there yet. That must have been the delay that allowed me to catch up.

The SUV pulled up as I appeared on the edge of the screen. Running. All the masked people looked my way. A few scrambled for the SUV's doors. I could see my mouth yell. But then the SUV took off with me chasing it.

I made him back up and pause. There it was. The rest of the license plate number: 6LIK723.

Grabbing a notepad on his desk, I jotted it down, ripped off the paper and stuffed it in my pocket. He pressed play again and, bloody hell, there was the footage of me trying to carjack some poor innocent soul. I'd forgotten all about that part of the night. Then the train blocked my way and I walked off.

"Whew. You did get it all."

"Yup." He grinned.

I peeled another three hundred dollars off a wad in my pocket. "You deserve this, but I'm going to need a copy of this to give to the police."

He drew back.

"What?"

"You want to give it to the police?"

"Well, sort of. Why, is that a problem?"

He shrugged, but looked uncomfortable. "They get really weird about drones recording things in public. You're not really supposed to ... privacy stuff."

I pried open his fingers, slapped the money into his palm and closed his fingers over it, holding my hand over his and meeting his eyes. "I protect my sources. I'll go to jail rather than give you up. Besides, the cop I'm working with, he's an old friend. He's cool. He'll do whatever I say." A little tiny white lie.

The guy shook his head.

"Please?"

He sat back down and fiddled with one of the computers. After a few seconds, he handed me a thumb drive. I could tell he wasn't very happy about it. Didn't really trust me. Yet.

"What's your name?"

"Danny."

"I owe you." I leaned over and scribbled my name and number on a piece of paper. "If you need help with something, I'm your girl."

It looked like he was about to say something but then he exhaled so much his bangs lifted an inch off his forehead then flopped back down. I headed toward the door.

"Pleasure doing business with you."

17

I LOVE IT HERE

I'd hardly stepped out of Danny's building before I dialed James.

"Something new?"

"I've got the plate." I knew I sounded smug.

Silence.

"How?" His voice was full of suspicion.

"Long story. Guy with drone recorded Sasha's abduction. Got a copy of the video, too."

James let out a low whistle. That's right, underestimate me, now be impressed.

"You at the police station?"

"Uh, my place. I'm home for the night."

A vivid memory of his overheated, spice-smelling manly apartment with him naked in the shower came roaring back to me. I swallowed.

"Gia?"

"Be there in ten."

My Uber driver was there in two. He was a Somalian with a ready smile.

"Howdy," I said as I hopped in.

"You live in Tenderloin?"

"Yes. I mean, no." I stuttered. "I'm moving here. Hopefully next month."

"Why?"

I looked out the window. There was a homeless guy I recognized walking by: a former boxer who owned an ancient golden lab named Max. He made sure Max was always fed, even before he ate. There was Chien Veit, my favorite place to grab Phở. On the corner, Larry, the manager of the Edgemont residential hotel, was out front sweeping the sidewalk. The next block over there was a monk in a long orange robe and bald head waiting for a bus. Across the street, a scruffy teenager with a Mohawk was playing his beat-up acoustic guitar and singing his heart out.

"Because," I finally told the driver. "I love it here."

I stood on the sidewalk in front of James' building for about five minutes before I got up the nerve to ring the buzzer. After the door clicked open, I crammed myself into the tiny elevator and hit the button for the fifth floor. When I stepped out, I saw that, like old times, the front door was propped open for me. An easel was set up against the window in his main room, displaying a half-finished painting of a beautiful woman in sunglasses, hair blowing back with the Golden Gate bridge looming behind her. A stab of jealousy zinged through me. Absurd.

Down the hall, in the tiny kitchen I could hear James puttering around. I closed and locked the front door and headed toward the smell of food.

"I'm sorry I've got to eat," he said over his shoulder. He was making scrambled eggs. Some sourdough toast popped out of the toaster. I started buttering them. The kitchen was so small he brushed up against me as he worked.

"You hungry?"

"I could eat."

A few minutes later we were sitting at the small café table on his tiny balcony, eating toast, scrambled eggs with cheese, and drinking white wine. He lived over by the ballpark in an obnoxiously expensive studio apartment with a view of the stadium and Bay Bridge.

Finally, he pushed his empty plate back.

"Sorry, I was starting to go brain dead. Hadn't eaten all day. I wasn't sure I could have a coherent conversation until I had some food."

"I get it." My plate was clean, too. "What's for dessert?"

He grinned, his dimple showing. "I'm glad to see that hasn't changed."

I shrugged.

He stood and gathered our plates, using his hip to open the sliding glass door.

"I'm gonna need more wine, too," I hollered after him.

Sitting on his balcony, I thought about how nice it was to have James for a friend. We got along great. It was only when he wanted to get serious with me that I had a problem. I could see us being friends for a long time. He really was a good guy. It was so much better this way, without any pressure.

After a dessert of chocolate chip cookies, we moved inside. Because it was a studio, his bedroom was his living room and vice versa. I tried to ignore the twin bed pushed up against the wall and faced the desk near his loveseat and took out the thumb drive.

He was silent as he watched the video on his computer monitor. Then swore under his breath.

"Okay. I need to make this official. I have to go to my sergeant."

Anger surged through me. "You promised me until Sunday."

His shoulders remained rigid.

"You promised."

I held my breath. He was a man of his word. That's why I had turned to him.

He let out an angry sound. But I knew I'd won. "I'm dead serious. Tomorrow night at six, I take this to my sergeant," he said. "It goes against everything I believe, but you're right—I promised you."

"Thank you." I leaned down and moved to give him a kiss on the cheek at the same time he turned his head and my lips met his.

I didn't come up for air again for quite a while, finding a nice spot on his lap. Pretty soon my top was unbuttoned and I had straddled him.

But then, thank God, his phone rang.

He glanced over at the desk and swore. "I have to take this."

I leaped off him. *Bobby. Bobby. Bobby.*

I held my shirt closed with one hand and watched James as he listened to whomever was speaking to him on the phone. He was smiling at me with those dimples and I can't lie—my heart melted a little.

But Bobby.

In reality, I thought Bobby had dumped me. But I wasn't quite sure. And wasn't that the entire point of our beef in the first place? That I wouldn't commit and become exclusive? That I refused to agree to avoid situations like the one I was in right now? So, why did I feel nearly sick with guilt?

Meanwhile, James gave me a look that would have melted me into a puddle before Bobby. Pre-Bobby. Before Bobby. BB.

James scooted his office chair over as he spoke into the phone. "Mmm hmmm. Yes. Sure."

I moved out of his reach and he raised his eyebrow.

"I'm so sorry," I mouthed, feeling even worse. I kissed my fingers and placed them on his cheek.

Grabbing my bag, I refused to look at him as I slunk down the hall to the front door. Part of me—a small petty part—noted that he didn't get off the phone to try to stop me.

Taking the stairs instead of the elevator, I felt increasingly lighter as the distance between us grew.

18

SPECIAL DELIVERY

INSTEAD OF TAKING AN UBER, I HOPPED THE BUS BACK TO MY PLACE AND walked up the steep hill from Columbus Avenue. I wanted to clear my head. The last tiny burst of the setting sun cast a smoky orange glow throughout my place and then darkness fell. I kicked off my shoes, flung open the doors to the balcony and leaned on the edge of my small wall, looking down at the city bustling below me on a Saturday night. The Golden Gate was lit up before me, making my heart clench with joy. For a girl who grew up in small town Monterey, living in the city had always been my dream. Unfortunately, it took my parents' murders to get me up here.

Padding into my kitchen in my socks, I poured some bourbon. The buzz of the wine at James' house had worn thin. There was no Django there to greet me and no Bobby on the other end of the phone line. I propped my feet up on my wall and sank into my cushioned chair on the balcony. I reached for my cigarettes but then threw them back down. Sitting in the dark, I went over everything I knew about Sasha's disappearance.

It wasn't adding up. There had to be something somewhere. Some clue to where she was and why she was taken. I grabbed my laptop and searched for information on King and the hate groups. There was so much online I didn't even know where to start. I wasn't very tech savvy. It was something I'd avoided despite my friends' derision. I didn't do Snapchat or Instagram or Facebook or Twitter. But tonight, after I took a shower, I'd search Sasha's social media accounts for clues and then Google the hell out of all my suspects.

Swallowing the last of my drink, I set aside my laptop and looked at the sky, watching white clouds floating past in the darkness lit up by a full moon.

In the shower, I let the hot water beat down on me, luxuriating in it. My body was alive, electric, tingling with desire. But not for James. For Bobby.

A dull ache filled in my gut whenever I thought about Bobby stomping out of my place.

With my hair wrapped in a white towel and nothing else on, I headed toward my living room where I'd left my phone. A tiny part of me wondered if there was some tiny drone out in the darkness filming me strutting around nude, but I had bigger things to worry about.

Picking up my phone, I scrolled to my favorites and dialed Bobby. The ringing seemed like a rebuke. Then, too soon, it went to voice-mail. Maybe it was better that way since I hadn't planned what to say. I glanced at the clock. Ten at night. Didn't he have to work in the morning? Jealousy like I'd never felt in my life surged through me. He was out with a girl. Or, God forbid, in bed with his new girlfriend. The thought made me hang up without leaving a message.

It was all my fault.

I was a jerk.

The buzzer from my doorman chirped and my heart jumped into my throat. Maybe Bobby was here. Downstairs. Right now. Maybe that's why he didn't answer his phone. He wanted to surprise me. I raced to the speaker by my door.

"Yes?"

"Miss Santella. You got a package here."

My heart sunk.

"You want me to send it up? I can give it to Jose. He was going up there anyway to water the plants."

"Sure." I knew I sounded dejected. Because I was.

A few minutes later, I'd thrown on a robe and there was a knock at the door.

I handed Jose a twenty in exchange for the small cardboard box. It was the size of a grapefruit. I closed the door and took it to my kitchen counter. There wasn't any address or marking on the box. Only some clear tape. I used a knife to slice through the tape and opened it.

Inside, a small black velvet jewelry box was nestled in Styrofoam peanuts.

What the hell? Despite myself, my childish romantic notions kicked in. Bobby sent me a piece of jewelry. He did love me.

My finger popped open the lid. I gasped and flung the box across the room, slumping on the floor. For a few seconds, I couldn't figure out what the god-awful noise in my apartment was. Then I realized it was me screaming. I clamped my mouth shut.

The box held a ring, all right.

A tiny ring attached to a tiny brown toe with a tiny pink-painted toenail.

When I finally could breathe properly again, I retrieved the cardboard box. A little slip of white paper was folded inside. It had been below the velvet box.

I grabbed my big oven mitts so I wouldn't leave fingerprints and opened it. The words were typed.

"We said no cops. You went to cops. Call them off. Now. Next time, it's her head."

Staring at the note, I couldn't breathe. I had done this. It was my fault. Someone had been following me. I couldn't get enough air in my lungs. I'd blown it.

19

EMANCIPATION

I USED MY OVEN MITTS TO PICK UP THE BLACK VELVET BOX, WHICH HAD snapped close when I flung it across the room. Thank God. The thought of hunting for Sasha's pinky toe somewhere in my apartment was unbearable. I put the box on the bookshelf in my living room. My hands were shaking like mad. My blood pounded in my ears and my face felt icy cold.

My first instinct was to call 911. But I couldn't go to the police. Going to the police was why Sasha's toe was in my living room.

I glanced at the clock. Eleven. I had nineteen hours to find Sasha before James took the kidnapping to his sergeant, which I was now certain would mean her death. I had to get my act together and do whatever it took to find Sasha.

I needed to get James off the case. Or at least pretend like I had. I reached for my phone. At first I hesitated. What if they had some tap on my phone? But then I shook it off. It was more likely someone had followed me to the precinct and to James' apartment.

Grabbing my phone, I shot James a text: "Sorry. I suck at relationships. Platonic is best. Any luck on the plate?"

It was the most pathetic apology ever, but at least this time I *had* apologized.

The little bubbles showed he was typing. I braced myself for a flurry of angry words about what a cold-hearted bitch I was, but instead he had taken the higher ground.

"Fire and ice."

I stared at the words for a minute before I realized he was talking about us and our chemistry. Oh yeah.

I texted a bitmoji of me with flames around me.

He texted back a bitmoji of him shivering.

I sent him a laughing-so-hard-crying bitmoji, which was the opposite of how I was feeling, and then typed, "The plate?"

"Retired woman-Indiana."

"? So not Mayor?"

I watched the little bubbles showing he was typing.

"Don't forget. Going to SGT at 6 p.m."

Panic coursed through me. I made a decision and typed quickly. "Onto something. Should have her soon."

"?"

I turned my phone on mute and set it down. It had taken all my willpower not to tell him about the pinky toe. I was so freaked out by it. Scared shitless for Sasha. Not telling the police went against all my instincts right then.

I decided that if things went south between now and noon, I would tell James about the toe and the threat. Or else I could lie. If I told him about the toe, the police investigation would take off like gangbusters and Sasha could very well end up dead. If I lied, I could stall.

For a second I considered calling Dante. His fiancé, Matt, had connections. Big time connections in Washington. Maybe it was time to look past our little corner of the world for answers. But would Matt know any dirt about the mayor? Maybe not. Besides, I knew Dante was probably asleep. He went to bed early every night so he could be awake at four in the morning to oversee the breakfast prep at his restaurant.

Giving my laptop a glance, I decided the pinky toe had been a game changer. I needed someone who knew more about online searching than how to google Thai takeout.

———

I PULLED up the collar of my All Saints motorcycle jacket as I stepped off the bus near Market Street into the fog surrounding the Forgotten Island. The area was almost always enveloped in its own island of fog, which I'd heard was how it got its name.

The streets were deserted and most of the lights were broken. Long shadows stretched across the streets. I hurried through the area, eager to get over to the Whoa-Man.

This time I was able to avoid the fire escape because when I walked up, the drone was hovering above me. I looked up and saw Danny's big red head hanging out the window.

"Hey."

"Hey," he said as if he were expecting me.

"Buzz me in," I demanded and without waiting for an answer headed under the small awning at the front door. Within thirty seconds the door clicked and I shoved it open. I took the stairs two at a time. The clock was ticking. Eighteen and a half hours left.

When I got to 10D and tried the handle it was locked. I knocked. And waited. I heard shuffling inside. I pressed my ear to the door and heard him swear.

Then the door flew open and I nearly fell inside.

I glanced around. How cute. He had cleaned up after he saw me downstairs. The closet inside the door was partly open and I could see he'd thrown clothes and food containers in there.

This time, I looked around his apartment as I followed him to the wall of computers. He had little bobble heads of most of the San Francisco Giant's players and a bookshelf full of Star Wars action figures, some still in the box.

"How old are you, anyway?"

A flush crept up the pale, freckled skin of his neck.

"Seventeen."

"Aw, you're just a baby." I smiled.

He looked down.

"A really, smart baby. Like a genius. A prodigy." I was making things worse. His cheeks were now bright red.

"Listen. I need your help again. It's really bad."

He looked over at me. I'm sure he heard the fear in my voice.

"They cut off my friend's pinky toe and sent it to me because they know I'm dealing with a cop. He's kept the lid on it, not telling his supervisors, but he is going to blow it out of the water at six tomorrow night. I need your help with a couple things."

He nodded, serious.

"I need to find out all the dirt on the mayor I can. He's somehow connected to all this. And I need to figure out who is following me. I thought maybe your drone could help with that last part and your tech savvy with the first."

He clamped his mouth together. He didn't seem convinced so I reached into my pocket where I had a wad of cash.

He held up his palm. Like his head, it was huge. He could palm my face.

"Wait."

I waited.

"I like to work on the barter system."

My body instantly tensed.

He spoke fast. "My petition for emancipation is on Wednesday. But I'm having trouble providing proof of income," he gestured at his bank of computers. "It's all under the table. I can't report it. Can't show proof."

I tilted my head, listening.

"And," he said, "You throw around cash like money isn't a thing for you."

"It's not." I said.

"Can you come with me and say I work for you?"

"To court?"

He gulped and nodded.

"Sure." I didn't hesitate.

"You'll lie to a judge?" He seemed surprised.

"Yeah. Seems like a good cause."

His big shoulders sagged with relief. "Thank you. I can't go back to my parent's house."

"Understood."

His face reddened a bit and he turned back to his keyboard. "What's Mayor McCheese's social security number?"

"No clue." Uh oh. This wasn't going to be easy.

He kept typing and I sighed with relief. When he wasn't looking, I put two hundred bucks on his table. I'd still show up Wednesday, but dude was doing me a service. I may be willing to lie to a judge for a good cause but I wasn't a freeloader. I paid for my goods.

Danny pushed back from the computer. "Here's the pre-primary report—money he's got so far."

I leaned over. It looked like a photo copy of a document that had been scanned. It said, "Campaign finance report of receipts and expenditures."

The first page showed that Mayor Evans had already received more than $500,000 nine months before the primary. Danny scrolled down to the actual spreadsheet listing donor names and amounts. Everything was sideways, so we tilted our heads. "You should look for the big donors first, right?"

"Yup," I said.

About half of the donations were $1,000, the maximum an individual could donate.

"Can you print this out?"

While the sheets came out, I dug around in my bag. I extracted a hot pink highlighter and marked the thousand dollar donations looking for some common thread.

There were a few that stood out. AKKI Industries. DKKI Corp. FKKI Construction. HKKI Specialist. LKKI Properties. PKKI Real Estate. RKKI Holdings. MKKI Imports. KKKI Trust. ZKKI LLC.

The letter before the KKI made sure they weren't lumped alphabetically together. Between them all, they added up to ten thousand dollars. Not a lot. But still.

Then I noticed another similar group. These ten donors followed the same pattern. But instead of KKI, the common factor was KJR. And there were more. In all, if they were all related, they added up to about $100,000. *That* was nothing to sneeze at.

By the time I looked up, it was three in the morning. Fifteen hours left.

Danny handed me a cup of coffee. At first I turned up my nose at it, but I was desperate for caffeine so I took a sip. "Not bad."

I flipped to the back of the papers, to the expenditures. Boring stuff. But I paused on rent. Why did the mayor pay rent on five different places in the Tenderloin?

"How do we get the addresses for these rentals?" I asked. Danny was slumped on his couch playing Minecraft on his TV.

He stood and stretched. "I'm on it." He ambled over to the computers and typed on one of the keyboards.

"Why do you have so many computers anyway?"

He looked at me for a second and then said, "I told you. My business."

"Okay."

I sucked down my coffee and used the bathroom. When I walked back into the main room, Danny held out a sheet with seven addresses. Six had the mayor's name by them. One, in Berkeley, said Kraig King. I shot a glance at Danny. Had I even mentioned King to him? I wasn't sure I had. I scanned the addresses again. They meant nothing to me. They were all in San Francisco on streets I recognized. Maybe I would need to go visit all of them.

"Can I use one of these computers?"

"Sure."

I sat down. Then noticed one of the six with the mayor's name on it had a star. "What's this?"

"His house in the avenues. His primary residence. Where he lives, you know, with his wife and kids."

He wouldn't be hiding Sasha there. I started on the other ones. While, I didn't know much about searching online I was an expert with Google maps. To my surprise, the rest were all here in the Tenderloin.

"Wow. The mayor is investing in the Tenderloin? Or at least renting spaces here for campaign activity?"

That explained his speedy arrival at Café Katrina's the night of the protest. Or maybe it didn't. "Want to go on a field trip?"

"Not really." He yawned.

"Do you think your drone could follow me as I check out these buildings?"

He shrugged.

For some reason, I didn't want to do it alone, even though I had my gun in my holster.

The Whoa-Man was the Tenderloin area furthest from my place. I could hit all the addresses on my way back to Russian Hill. I marked them in order so I wouldn't backtrack on my walk home.

I'd hit one address in the Gimlet, one in Delicious Fields, one in the Panhandle, one in the Rambles, and the last one in the Forgotten Island.

Danny was already fiddling with his drone. It took center stage on his huge dining room table in the middle of the room.

"The battery's almost dead."

"Crap."

"If you walk fast, it might hold out."

"Okay. I can do that." I grabbed my bag, shoved the papers in it and headed to the door. "Thanks a lot. I'll be there Wednesday morning."

20

GIMLET

When I stepped outside, I looked up and saw Danny leaning out the window. The drone was in the air nearby. I blew him a kiss. I could practically see him blush from ten stories down.

The streets were silent so I could hear the slight buzz of the drone above me although I couldn't see it.

The first address, about two blocks away, led me to a small building in the Gimlet. The shades were drawn but a large "Evans for Mayor" sign took up most of the window. It looked official. And like a campaign office.

The second address in Delicious Fields was a little more confusing. It was a small four-story building. I was ninety-nine percent sure the apartments inside were SRO's. Cheap little single residency occupancy apartments. Could you write off the rental of an apartment for your campaign staff? I didn't have a clue. It seemed a little odd. I glanced down at my sheet. Yeah, the mayor had paid only $800 for the first three months of this year. Suspicious.

The next address in the Panhandle was another apartment building that looked like another SRO. Did the mayor have a string of kept women in the Tenderloin?

The Panhandle was my old neighborhood, soon to be my home

again. Passing Café Katrina, I wanted nothing more than to swing in and give Katrina a hug and down a bourbon, but every minute counted. James was going to his sergeant in mere hours.

I stopped to peruse the construction on my new home. I couldn't wait to move back. From the outside, the place looked finished, but when I'd gone by the other day, they were still working on the interior. For every tenant who had lived in the building before it burned down, I'd doubled the size of their original apartment. For my penthouse apartment, I was having the contractor put in some special touches.

Like my old place, there would be a staircase to the roof within my apartment. But the door would be hidden. I would train Django how to use his nose to trigger the door if he needed to do his business on the roof when I wasn't home.

In any case, the roof was going to be my safe haven. It would contain fruit trees and a garden much like the rooftop being designed at Swanson Place. But my roof would also have had a few special turrets I could fire from in case all hell broke loose in the city. You never knew.

In my penthouse, I had smart windows installed on all three sides. The windows not only had tint but also were made of bulletproof glass. The open layout of my floor was mainly so I had a big room to do my karate. As soon as I moved in I was going to start training again hard. That would also mean giving up booze and smoking for a while. Living in my Russian Hill apartment had led to me falling back on bad habits.

My new place also had reinforced steel doors and a safe room tucked away in case someone did manage to get through that door. Unlikely. My safe room was grand central for the building's security system that would allow me to put the entire building on lock down with the flick of a button. More than a dozen surveillance cameras were strategically hidden around the exterior and roof. Standing on the sidewalk, even though I had planned where each security camera was mounted, I smiled when I confirmed I couldn't spot them.

While I was looking up at the building, I hadn't paid much attention to a homeless woman walking toward me. When I looked over at her, I gasped. For a second, I thought she was Ethel. This woman also had a scarf on her head. But unlike Ethel's it was flowered. And she wasn't black. She was white.

"Hey sister," I said.

"Got any change."

I dug around and found a twenty. "You ever want to change your situation? Live in an apartment?"

I was always recruiting for Swanson Place. Feeling people out, trying to get the perfect mix of residents.

She frowned. "Why?"

"I know of a place. You could work downstairs in the building. There's a bunch of shops."

"I don't want to work." She cackled.

"You might like it."

"Doubt that."

She turned to go.

"Hey, what's the word on the streets? I hear some people are vanishing, gone missing."

She rotated her pointy jaw toward me. "That's true."

"Are you worried?"

She thought about it a second and then shook her head. "Nah. They only want the blacks."

When I got to the address in the Rambles, my eyes were blurred from lack of sleep, but then I did a double take. 12 Eddy Street. Fuck me!

I looked up at the building as I dialed James. But as soon as he answered, I hung up. If I was wrong, Sasha would die. They'd warned me about bringing the police into this in a way I'd never forget. I couldn't take the chance. I dialed Baumann instead.

He sounded sleepy.

"I think I know where she is. She had some scribblings on her calendar that said 12 Eddy. I just found out the mayor owns a building at 12 Eddy and her story concerns the mayor. She's got to be here somewhere." I spoke fast, my words tumbling over one another.

"How sure are you?"

I swallowed. "Not sure enough to call the police."

Quickly, I filled Baumann in on the toe.

He was quiet when I finished.

"I'll meet you at the Black Panther in thirty minutes," he said.

21

BLACK PANTHER

As I made my way to the Black Panther, a buzzing near my ear made me jump. It was the drone. It had dropped down by me, startling me so much I yelped. I'd totally forgotten about it.

It hovered a few feet above me as if trying to tell me something. It started to go away and then came back. What did it want me to do? Then I remembered: The battery. I gave a thumbs up and that must have been the right thing to do because it zoomed away and was soon out of sight.

The Black Panther, a dark, dive bar with sticky floors and chairs, was mostly empty. Only a few diehards slumped at the bar.

I ordered a tap beer while I waited, figuring I better keep my wits about me.

Baumann came in wearing a trench coat with his jeans and cowboy boots.

I eyed the boots. They were made of snake skin and dyed black cherry. "Those are kick ass."

"Ready?"

It was misting as we walked and I pulled my jacket collar up and tucked my chin into my scarf. Finally, the building appeared in the low-hanging fog.

We stood under the awning and looked at all the doorbell buttons. There were eight apartments.

"Start ringing doorbells?"

Baumann said, "Might as well."

I pressed the first button and nothing happened. I did it three more times and then raised an eyebrow. "Okay. On to number two."

This time the door buzzed and clicked open.

Baumann held the door, looking at me over his glasses. I took a deep breath and stepped inside. I gestured at the first apartment on the left. There were two apartments on each floor. "I'll start here."

The man who opened the door of number one was bleary eyed. I felt bad. He'd been sleeping.

"Excuse me? I'm sorry to wake you."

"*No hablo inglés.*"

Baumann was by my side in a second speaking to the man in Spanish. When they got done talking, the man stood there yawning while Baumann translated.

"He works nights. Says he doesn't know who owns the building and he has never seen a girl who looks like Sasha here. All the other residents are single guys like him from Mexico who work in restaurants. Most work two restaurant jobs so they're basically here to sleep for a few hours when they're not working. It's a really quiet building. He said he'd have heard something if a girl had been here."

"Can you ask him what time most of them get home?"

Baumann spoke quickly in Spanish. The man answered and Baumann turned to me.

"He said he's usually the earliest one home after the restaurant closes at one."

According to her calendar, Sasha was supposed to meet King here at midnight. The building might have been empty.

"Can we trust him?" I said it, but I already knew the answer.

Baumann didn't hesitate. "Yeah."

I looked at my watch. It was four in the morning. Fourteen hours left to find Sasha.

"Then I'm not sure it's worth knocking on all these doors," I said.

"I don't want to wake people up for nothing. Sounds like most of them have to get up in a few hours."

"Check the basement. I'll check the roof," he said.

The basement was a small space, mostly taken up by the stairs. There were five bicycles chained to a pole, including a bright red one that looked new. A door was at one end. I turned the handle and found a janitor's closet.

Baumann was coming down the stairs when I got to the lobby.

"Door to the roof is locked from this side. Probably illegal and a fire hazard. If these guys went to the roof to get away from fire, they'd be in trouble." He sounded angry.

"I guess I'm not surprised the mayor is an absentee slumlord." I was angry, too, and not only about that. This whole exercise was a waste of everybody's time.

A dead end. I'd wasted precious hours that should've been spent finding Sasha.

"What next, boss?" Baumann said.

"Ha." But I thought about it. "I have an address for King. It's in your town. You mind swinging by there on your way home to see if anything seems suspicious."

"Sounds good." He started to walk away and then turned back.

"Hey, it was a good lead. We needed to check it out."

I shrugged. He smiled and headed toward the Powell Street BART station.

Baumann was cool about it, but I could tell he'd wished he'd stayed home in his nice warm bed.

22

TRUE WARRIOR

FEELING DEJECTED, I STARTED OUT TOWARD RUSSIAN HILL. I WOULD hit the last address on my walk home. I stepped onto Mason Street, the unofficial border to the Forgotten Island part of the Tenderloin. But I would've known the difference. It was as if this neighborhood had a darkness that surrounded it. I remembered the creepy feeling I had the other day around there.

The streetlights were broken and the entire area felt remote and forlorn, even though I knew less than a block away Market Street was bustling.

Glancing at my sheet of paper, I read the address: 240 Turk Street. I squinted in the near darkness to see if I could spot a building with an address. Most of the buildings didn't have addresses, which was another bizarre aspect of the Forgotten Island.

Nearly all the buildings were abandoned with boarded-up windows and doors.

The building closest to me had half of an address 23 ... So, I knew I was close. I found another numbered building and that's when I looked up.

The address matched. It was the abandoned building that had given me the creeps the other day. But now as the fog cleared, it didn't look abandoned. The twelve-foot-high chain link fence was shiny. Getting closer, I examined the lock on the gate. New. I glanced up at the windows. If someone were inside with some type of light I would never know. The windows were black with curtains or shades or something else.

The rumble of a vehicle nearby sent me scrambling. I raced across the street and ducked into a deep dark doorway of an old liquor store with the sign hanging from one bolt. Tucked in there I knew I was invisible. I pressed myself against the wall as the vehicle's headlights turned onto the street, briefly flashing my way. The far reaches of the beam glanced against my boot, which I pulled back even further into the shadows.

The vehicle rolled into sight. It was a black SUV. My heart thudded. The driver got out to unlock the gate, but it was on the other side of my vantage point, so I couldn't see him or her, only a dark figure. I stretched my neck out, but couldn't get a glimpse of the license plate from my hiding spot unless I stepped out into the street. I shrunk back into the doorway: another car was coming down the road.

A black sedan with dark tinted windows stopped right in front of me and waited for the SUV to enter the fenced parking lot. The SUV pulled into the parking lot, followed by the sedan. A passenger— someone all in black—jumped out and locked the gate behind the two vehicles. A huge garage door creaked open and the vehicles disappeared inside. Before the door closed, I glimpsed a metal staircase across a vast open and empty space.

Once again, I eyed the fence. If it weren't for the barbed wire dangling down on my side, I would scale that baby in a second and go snoop around.

Meanwhile, I'd wait to see if the vehicles came out any time soon. I glanced at my phone. Past five in the morning. Which also meant thirteen hours until James was going to his superiors, putting Sasha's neck on the line. Damn it.

Sasha's disappearance was connected to the mayor and a black SUV and this building was connected to both. I was right where I needed to be.

It is during those times when all seems to be lost that the true warrior digs deep down inside and finds his true strength and purpose. He will unerringly know when he is doing what is right and true and just.

By dawn, I was crunched in the corner of the doorway, numb and cold and stiff, barely able to keep my eyes open. That's when I heard a screech and opened my eyes in time to see both vehicles pulling out of the gate. This time I could see the driver. He looked military. His hair was shorn and he wore all black clothing and sunglasses even though the sky was only now beginning to lighten. He was nondescript. Indistinguishable in any way. Completely average.

If I saw him again, I wouldn't recognize him. Instead, I stared at the back window of the sedan as it rolled past. Was the mayor inside?

My phone buzzed right then and I looked down at the text that appeared. Baumann.

"King place quiet. Will wait til 7."

"Thx," I texted back.

I felt helpless. Sitting back, watching and spying was not helping us find Sasha. Unless she was in the building. Something they wanted to hide was in that building. The fence and padlocked gate made that apparent. Besides the garage door, there were no other obvious ways to enter the building. All the doors were boarded up.

Feeling desperate, I did something probably foolish. I stepped out into the street after the sedan had passed, standing in the middle of the road. The vehicles were three blocks away, but I saw the brake lights flash once before I stepped back into the shadows.

Come on. Come back. I would throw myself in the passenger door. I would pretend to be hit by the car. I would try all the doors on the car. Anything to see if the mayor and his smug face was sitting in the back seat. I waited but the car didn't stop. The rumble of the vehicles grew distant and then disappeared.

23

EVIL, DARK SHIT

EVEN THOUGH I'D INTENDED TO HEAD HOME AND SLEEP A FEW HOURS, IT now seemed like a waste. I didn't have time for that. Instead, I headed to Darling's salon. I found her in the back. She looked a little more presentable than the last time I'd seen her. Her hair was back on her head in silky black curls and her Cleopatra eyes were made up to perfection.

Django ignored me. He probably thought I'd abandoned him and that he was now Darling's dog. Hell, maybe he was. When I first walked in, he'd looked up with interest and then put his head back down on his paws and closed his eyes. I couldn't blame him. I was terrible at relationships. Even the dog knew.

Darling was on the couch sipping coffee and watching the morning news.

"Where's Precious?" I asked, narrowing my eyes suspiciously.

"She's sleeping in at my place. She'll be here, soon."

I told her what I'd learned about the mayor's business holdings in the Tenderloin, hoping she might be able to shed some insight.

She looked off in the distance, thinking. This was the old Darling I knew. The strong, smart woman who'd grown a multi-million-dollar business from nothing.

"Sasha wrote a story that was going to ruin the mayor, so he must be behind her disappearance—is that what you're saying?"

"That's what I think."

"Have you gone to his house?"

"I haven't," I admitted. "But only because I know he lives there with his wife and kids and I think it's unlikely he'd let any of his other activities near them. But it probably wouldn't hurt to have someone go there and put a tail on him."

Mentally, I kicked myself for not thinking of this earlier.

I hid my shame by pulling my mug of coffee to my face and taking a long sip. When I put the mug down Darling was staring at me with wide eyes.

"I spent last night awake lying in bed thinking of everything Sasha said to me the past two weeks. I was trying to remember every word. I don't know, but I think maybe all the people disappearing lately in the Tenderloin, I think she was also looking into that."

"Go on." I sat up straighter.

"When I was concerned about the missing people she said, 'Nonna, don't worry I'm working on a story that makes sure these people never hurt anyone again.'"

Missing black homeless or poor. All from the Tenderloin. A fake Antifa group. Kraig King. The mayor and his re-election campaign. Sasha's story to ruin the mayor.

What was the connection? Was the mayor behind the disappearances? I had a hard time believing even a scumbag like him would stoop that low. Unless it was some Good Samaritan program where he was taking them off the streets and transplanting them somewhere like Swanson Place. *My* idea.

But if that were the case, he would be blabbing it all over the city. Every TV station would feature Evans and his bushy gray eyebrows. If I knew anything about the mayor, it was that he was the quintessential politician. Every move was calculated and geared to boost and bolster his public image. From the make-up he wore at the gym (in case there was a photo op) to the finely tailored blazers he wore to stroll the beach, the mayor was all about the promotion machine.

Thinking of Sasha's pinky toe back on my dining room table, I had a hard time believing he would either participate in, or condone, violence of that caliber. One time, he'd been asked to give a statement about a severed hand found floating in the Bay. When a reporter had shown him a picture of it, he'd visibly cowered and turned green, looking as if he were trying not to vomit. He found the world's dark underbelly, which included the Tenderloin, distasteful.

The pinky toe.

Of course, I'd avoided telling Darling that detail. I couldn't, because deep down inside I knew I had caused it. By going to the police I'd effectively maimed her precious grandbaby. She had been so against me going to the cops in the first place. I'd made a colossal mistake.

The only way I could possibly make up for it would be to bring Sasha home safely. Darling was watching me after I finished speaking. I'd become lost in my own thoughts. She was looking at me as if I held the secret keys to the kingdom. It was too much.

But I had made her a promise. I shook off my fears and doubts and thought about what we knew again. At the core of it all was someone's desire to stop Sasha from running a story in the newspaper. But what was the story?

"This is all an effort to kill Sasha's story. But what they don't seem to know is that the editor doesn't even have the story. I don't want to tell her kidnappers that we don't even have the story because then any leverage we have is gone. Baumann says Sasha never filed it. It's probably somewhere on her laptop, which is missing." I stood and looked around the office. "Darling, did she ever mention places she worked, maybe a coffee shop where she took her laptop to write or something like that?"

Darling scrunched up her face thinking. "She sometimes brought her laptop here if she was writing on deadline," Darling pointed to a small desk. "And one time she brought it here to help me with some computer stuff. I'd forgotten to save and then spilled some water on my computer. Lost the whole darn file."

"That's the worst."

"Yes, but my grandbaby is so smart. She showed me how to use her Dropbox to make sure everything I did was saved."

I froze. Sasha used Dropbox. I tried not to get too excited.

"Do you guys share a Dropbox account?"

"Yes," Darling said. "Why?" And then she leaped to her feet as she realized. "Oh, Lordy! It might have her story!"

Within seconds, Darling had logged in to her computer and then the Dropbox account.

The fourth file down was Sasha's. It was labeled "Sunday Story."

That was it.

I closed my eyes and said a little prayer to a God I wasn't even sure I believed in. Then we clicked on the file, opened it, and read, sitting side-by-side. Darling read out loud in a low murmur.

At the end, we both sat back stunned.

"Oh, sweet Jesus. Sasha got herself mixed up in some evil, dark shit."

24

DOWN-AND-OUT

"*IF THEY COME FOR ME IN THE MORNING, THEY WILL COME FOR YOU IN THE night.*" — Angela Y. Davis

————

THIS QUOTE WAS at the top of Sasha's story. According to her sources, the mayor was raking in stupendous campaign contributions from shell companies run by King, whose full name was Kraig Kristopher King, Jr.

It all made sense. Sasha was supposed to meet King that night. KKK.

He owned dozens of companies under two business names: Kraig King Industries and Kraig King Jr. All the shell companies I had seen in the mayor's campaign contributions all had either KKI or KKJ in them.

In return for the financial payoff, King had promised to "help" the mayor "clean up" the Tenderloin, as the mayor promised in his campaign platform. Sasha had an off-the-record source confirming this. In other words, King's men were murdering the downtrodden people of color in the Tenderloin.

While Sasha's story stated there was no proof that the mayor about the methods used to clean up "aka ethnic cleansing," she had other people saying there was no way the mayor hadn't known. I agreed.

King had targeted the down-and-out people in the Tenderloin. The homeless. The poor. But only if they were people of color. It was so evil it didn't seem real. But I knew it was.

A warrior's rage must always be directed toward fighting for that which is right and just and not as a reaction to a personal battle.

My blood was boiling.

These fuckers were targeting the weakest and most vulnerable people in our city. Many of the homeless people I knew ended up on the streets because something stood in the way of their access to resources for addiction and mental illness. Sure, there were a few who made choices that led them there and were the bad eggs, but they were the minority on the streets.

Darling was holding her heart when we finished reading the story.

I turned toward her computer again. "Do you mind?"

She just nodded.

"Thanks," I said. "I'll just be a few minutes. I'm going to send out a few emails about what we found."

After I was done, I told Darling I had to run, but would be back in touch soon.

"You bring back my grandbaby." She was furious. Her patience was spent. I didn't blame her. Time was running out.

Outside the salon, I called James. The street sounds, the trains, the cars, the people, made it hard to hear, but I welcomed the distraction. It would make my story believable.

"We found her. Thanks for all your help. I'm so sorry to bother you. It was all a big misunderstanding. I'm about to step into the BART station, so I might lose you. You know how college kids are. She was off with a boy.

I cringed at my lie and for making Sasha seem so flaky. But it was necessary.

After rambling, I waited. It was silent.

"James?"

"I don't believe you." He didn't sound angry, but his voice was firm.

"That's crazy. You have to believe me." I shot a frantic look around. I could grab that homeless woman and pay her to talk. "Want me to put her on the phone?" It would be a huge gamble. The homeless woman probably sounded like she was one hundred years old and might even go off script. I held my breath.

"I've got a better idea." He sounded so smug. I closed my eyes.

"Why don't you send me a picture, a selfie of you guys together. Maybe even do a Facetime with me ..."

I cut him off. "James? The BART train is coming. I'm having a hard time hearing you. James?" I rubbed my sweater across the phone. "Are you there? If you can hear me, here's the plan: I'll meet you at my apartment at eight. If you can hear me still, plan on being there—we're having a celebratory dinner and you can meet her yourself."

Without waiting for an answer, I clicked off. I stared at the fog rolling into the Forgotten Island in the distance. I was going to need every second to find Sasha. If James believed me—in other words if I was really, really lucky—I'd just bought myself an extra two hours.

But I'd never been lucky.

25

THE FORGOTTEN ISLAND

EVEN THOUGH SOMEWHERE IN SAN FRANCISCO THE SUN HAD RISEN, THE Tenderloin remained dark and gray, saturated in a thick, low-lying fog that obscured any structure more than a block away.

I pulled up the collar of my leather jacket and suddenly my lack of sleep from the night before hit me. My head swam and I felt dizzy with fatigue. I stumbled a little over a crack in the sidewalk and caught myself. A woman with a briefcase gave me an odd look. Finally, I stepped into the Forgotten Island neighborhood. The building loomed before me like an ominous specter. The misty fog drifted before me. Every few seconds, an eerie breeze would part the fog, momentarily revealing the building.

I was grateful for the Forgotten Island's permanent layer of fog. It would provide cover. I eyed the fence, walking along it and looking up. The corner was my spot. There was a thick metal pole there. In addition, the fence dropped down a little there before it disappeared into the wall of the building. I shrugged off my jacket and started to climb.

When I neared the top where the coiled barbed wire fence bent toward me, I wrapped my arm in my thick leather jacket and tried to swat at it. It bent a little but sprung back. Grabbing my multi-purpose tool with one hand out of my jacket pocket, I unfolded the needle nose plier attachment, which was supposed to work as a wire cutter. I pressed as hard as I could and basically put a little crimp in the barbed wire. Then I took out my serrated knife and hacked at it. It merely scratched the wire. That's when I realized I wasn't dealing with your ordinary run of the mill barbed wire. Time for Plan B.

Unwrapping my arm, I shook out my jacket, and, holding on with one hand, swung it up and over the barbed wire. It stuck. Perfect.

Pulling myself up above the fence, I swung my leg over onto my jacket and straddled the barbed wire. As I shifted to swing my other leg over, tiny needles poked through my jacket into my flesh. Pain shot down my leg and I jumped, nearly flying off the fence. I managed to get both legs to the other side and still hold on. I clutched at my jacket and the barbs pierced my palms. Getting a firm grip on a piece of fence at the level of my torso, I tugged on my jacket trying to free it from the barb wire. It didn't budge.

I yanked on it again, clinging to the fence with one hand, my knuckles and fingers aching. I heard ripping. Just a little more. I jerked it one last time and the jacket broke free, but it sent me plunging to the ground. At the last minute, I tucked and rolled on the cement, landing on my shoulder. My arm was screaming in pain. I closed my eyes, biting back tears and pressing it to my side. With my other hand, I gingerly probed the skin, tendons, and bones with my fingers. I gasped from the pain, but was relieved. It had taken the brunt of my fall, but it didn't feel broken. The gun at the holster in my back had most likely left a gun-shaped bruise on my skin, but I'd survive that too. Good thing I had on a thick sweatshirt under my leather jacket. Tugging on my jacket, my first stab at getting my arm through the armhole was excruciating as my sore arm got tangled in the tattered and shredded remnants of the lining. The second time it slid through. Even so, the effort hurt like hell.

Then I remembered my phone. I reached into my pocket. It was shattered. I tried to hit the home button and nothing happened.

I darted toward the garage door. I had no idea how I was going to get in from there. As I sprinted, I realized my ankle was jacked up from the fall, as well, so I hobbled at a fast walk. The wind kicked up swirling dried leaves around my feet in mini whirlwinds, lifting them eerily so they became eye level. I swatted at the leaves as I ran and swore under my breath.

This place gave me the creeps. The wind whistled around a corner and I nearly screamed. I pressed myself against the cold building and looked for a way in. Then I spotted it. The plywood on the nearest window was screwed on. I took out my multi-purpose tool again and flicked open the screwdriver attachment and plucked the screws out one by one. Then I pried the board off and set it to one side. Beneath it was a half-broken window, jagged with glass. I reached down and lifted the glass out of the sill and set it aside. Kneeling, I peered into the building. The darkness stretched forever and made me want to turn and run.

I wiggled on my butt through the window, stretching with my legs to feel the floor. Nothing but air. Twisting, I propped my chest on the window and dropped, hoping there was floor below and that I wasn't dropping into the center of the earth. But it was only a few feet down and my feet landed with a soft thud.

I froze listening. For a second I imagined a heavy breathing, like how a bear or hell hound would sound, but I knew it was all in my mind, that there was nothing there. In the distance, I heard the ding of pipes. Then a rhythmic dripping sound. And beyond that, a very low, nearly inaudible sound that sent shivers down my spine. It sounded like moaning. I knew it wasn't and that my imagination was playing tricks on me, but my mouth instantly dried up and I found it difficult to swallow.

There was a small square of dim light that was coming in from the open window. I'd been so careful to cover my tracks, but leaving the plywood off the window would alert anyone who pulled up—anyone who was paying attention that is–that someone was inside.

I kicked my shoe around to see if there was anything I could stand on to try to at least pull the plywood over the window to look as if it were still intact, but my foot struck empty air. I scooted to the side so I was out of the dim square of light and in the shadows. I reached for my gun and unsnapped my holster with a loud click accompanied by a squeak from the holster's leather. I pressed my back to the wall and listened, waiting for my eyes to adjust.

The first floor was dark and felt about thirty degrees colder than the chill outside. I didn't hear anything unusual, but I couldn't help the tangible feeling of malevolence in the air. My rational mind told me that the room was empty. Of people. But my gut told me *something* was in the room.

Dread crawled up my spine and over my scalp as if someone had run a long pointy finger across my body. Somewhere deep in the depths of the building there was that sound again—a low murmur, nearly a moaning, that I decided must be the wind seeping in through cracks in the old building.

My eyes focused and darker shadows became distinguishable from lighter shadows. When I had been spying from the doorway across the street, I thought I'd caught a glimpse of what looked like a staircase inside the garage. I headed that way, keeping my gun in front of me and my back to the wall. When the wall disappeared behind me and I touched the garage wall, I knew the stairs were in front of me. But that meant leaving the safety of the wall and walking into the open dark, dank space. I closed my eyes and took a few deep breaths.

When I opened my eyes again, it seemed as if I could see a tiny bit better. Clutching my gun with both hands, I walked into the darkness, every nerve of my body on edge waiting for the gun to be yanked out of my hands or for it to smack into a solid body waiting for me in the dark. In the back of my mind, I vividly imagined every scary movie where the victim is stumbling along in the dark while some form of evil is watching her calmly and patiently with night vision goggles. I froze and listened. No heavy breathing. No shuffling of zombie-type feet toward me. So far so good.

And then that goddamn moaning started up again somewhere in the building. Okay. It was far away. I could handle anything as long as it wasn't here with me right now. I decided to take ten steps and then pause to listen. I counted the steps and then stopped.

Nothing. Not a sound. The building was enormous, so I had no idea how close I was to the stairs. I took five more steps. Nothing. I listened but only heard a weird metal clanking noise that sounded like it was coming from outside and not anywhere in the building. A murmur of voices outside and the growl of a motor vehicle sent my heart beating up into my throat right when the garage door squeaked loudly and began to rise. The light filtering in illuminated a metal staircase in front of me and I ran for it as if my life depended on it. Which it probably did.

Scaling the metal stairs, which creaked loudly at each step, I was up three stories where the stairs dead-ended before the garage door fully opened. Two doors lay before me. I tried the handle of the first one. It was locked. The second one opened onto an enclosed stairway. With lights. Flickering horror movie lights. But lights.

Behind me, the garage door shut with a bang. I stepped inside the inner staircase. It seemed to go up several stories. I had no choice but to head to the next floor. Except there wasn't one. It wasn't until two flights later that there was a door. It looked like solid steel. I tried the handle. It pushed open.

Slowly, I eased my foot into the space and listened. I heard a humming noise. I waited and when nothing happened, I pushed the door open a little more and then, crouching, stuck one eye to the opening. It was dark, but not as pitch black as the first floor. This time light from outside filtered in to a big cavern of a space. I slipped my body through the crack in the door and then carefully closed it behind me so it wouldn't make any noise.

Huge sheets of thick plastic were hung between giant pillars, sectioning the floor off into smaller spaces.

Grasping my gun, I headed toward the first area. If I didn't find Sasha here, I'd try the next floor and the next until I'd searched the entire building. And if she wasn't here? I glanced at my watch. It was now six in the morning. Twelve hours left.

Holding my breath, I stepped around the first sheet of thick plastic. Nothing. I moved onto the next. It wasn't until the fourth section that I found something. At first I stared, not sure what I was looking at in the dim light. Two long rows of giant plastic barrels. The ones closest to me didn't have lids on them and were empty. But there were about nine with lids tightly sealed. And then nearby, there were enormous containers stacked on top of one another. They contained clear liquid and had spigots.

Squinting in the dusty light I tried to read the label but it was too dark.

A bone-rattling rumble made me freeze. When I heard the distinct ding of an elevator, I jerked my head and saw a small light across the room from me. A freight elevator. I ducked into the furthest corner of the room behind the barrels with the lids on them. I pulled my legs in and made myself as small as possible as the elevator doors open with a whoosh. A series of lights overhead flickered on. A man grunted. "This guy has got to be at least 250 pounds." He sounded out of breath.

"That's what pisses me off," another voice said. "This guy begging for my hard-earned cash and he probably eats better than me. Probably getting all sorts of money from the government to sit around and drink all day."

"Yep. Total bullshit."

"I'm glad he decided to ... uh, take us up on our offer."

The other man laughed. "Dumb ass. Didn't his mama ever teach him there ain't nothing for free?"

"Are you kidding me? They don't teach them nothing but how to get one over on the system."

"Not for long. Not with King in charge. All that shit is going to change. Can't happen soon enough."

My heart stopped. These were King's henchmen. Killing the homeless. Here was proof. If only my phone wasn't out of commission I could have evidence. Or call for the police to come interrupt them in the act. But that wouldn't lead me to King. He was the big fish.

"This is good right here."

I heard a squishy thud and crack. I closed my eyes. I didn't have to have x-ray vision to know that they'd dropped this man's body on the cement floor, cracking the guy's head like an egg. If he wasn't already dead, he'd surely be dead now.

"Grab that one."

More grunting. "The dolly's over there."

I heard the squeak of wheels and more grunting.

Then the sound of liquid rushing into a container.

"Dude! Put on your mask." The voice was muffled.

"I got gloves on. Besides, they didn't wear masks in Breaking Bad."

"Okay, fuckwad, don't put on your mask. See if I give a shit."

I heard swearing and muffled voices.

After a few more minutes the sound of liquid stopped and I heard a snap that was probably the lid being pressed onto the plastic container.

"Let's get out of here," one man said. "This place gives me the creeps."

The other man laughed and shortly after I heard the sound of the elevator ding.

After the lights were flicked off and I heard the whoosh of doors opening and closing and the rumble of the elevator grew fainter, I dared to stand.

The liquid in the containers had to be hydrofluoric acid. I'd watched Breaking Bad. Binge watched it a few times, actually. Hydrofluoric acid liquefied bodies.

Walking past the barrels with plastic lids, which now numbered ten, I felt sick.

These men were treating people like slabs of meat.

And what was possibly even worse is that there were another few dozen barrels empty. Waiting.

I paused.

Bile filled my throat. What if Sasha was in one of these barrels. I looked around. I would need a tool to pry them open and even then, I would also need gloves and a mask or something to protect me if the liquid splashed out or I inhaled it.

I tried to remember how many people Darling and Kato had said were missing.

Not ten.

26

HUMAN WASTE

I DUCKED BACK INTO THE STAIRWAY, FEELING SAFE AGAIN FOR THE FIRST time in twenty minutes. It was apparent I was the only person using the stairs in this hell hole. Probably why the flickering lights had never been fixed. I hurried up two more flights to get to the next floor. This door was locked. I pushed and pulled and it didn't budge. The door handle on the next floor turned easily. I cracked the door half an inch, waiting. And then an inch. And then two inches. This floor was lit up. Afraid somebody was inside, I got my gun out and holding it close poked my head around the door. Something smelled bad. Like sweat and human waste.

The first thing I saw was a large desk in a corner with a computer on it. Squeezing through the small space, I stepped inside, keeping my foot in the door in case I needed to quickly escape. That's when I saw her.

Sasha was huddled on a mattress on the floor in the corner, sleeping. A metal cuff around her ankle led to a chain bolted into a wall. A large bandage on that foot was soiled and dirty. A jug of water was nearly empty. A few orange rinds were on a small plate and a giant tub had been used for waste. She moaned and turned. Her eyes were closed. Her long lashes resting on her cheekbones. I was hoping she was asleep and dreaming and not feverish from infection.

I quickly took in my surroundings. Besides the door to the stairs there was an elevator. Good. I wasn't sure how well she could walk with her injured foot. The chain to the wall would be a problem. I took out my multi-tool but I didn't think it would do the trick. I needed something bigger.

Deciding that it would be better if I woke her after I was ready to free her, I headed toward the desk and searched the drawers. The top drawer had the key to the shackle. I could hardly believe it. Maybe a lifetime of bad luck had turned. As I thought that, the elevator dinged. I didn't even have time to crouch behind the desk in a lame attempt to hide.

Instead I stood wide-eyed as Kraig King stepped out of the elevator. He gave me a slow smile that sent a chill down my spine. He wore a white shirt and white jeans and was flanked by two men with shaved heads wearing black. I scowled at them all. Up close, King was eerily tall. His watery eyes blinked as if it were difficult for him to see in the bright lights. That's when I noticed what had seemed so strange about him at Katrina's. His eyes were pinkish blue. Without the fedora, I saw his hair was white blond and swept up in an old-fashioned pompadour. He was an albino. That's why in public he always wore a fedora and dark sunglasses. I couldn't take my eyes off him. He was both strikingly handsome and terrifying at the same time.

King, obviously used to people gawking, ignored my open mouth and pointed up to the ceiling where I saw the red flashing light of a camera. I nodded, conceding my mistake.

Meanwhile, I tucked the key to the manacle into the back pocket of my jeans at the same time I reached for my gun tucked into my back waistband.

"Tssskkk tsssk tsssk" King said shaking his head. The two men in black raised assault rifles and pointed them at my face. I came away with my hands empty and palms in the air.

"Good girl."

"I don't suppose I need to ask what you're doing here?" he said.

I wanted to keep their attention off Sasha, who had sat up and was rubbing her eyes. He stared at me so I gave him a full-blown smile.

"Fuck you."

Before I realized it, he'd taken three long strides and slapped my cheek so hard I was sent flying into the desk chair. Stunned.

His goons yanked my gun out of my waistband and wrapped a rope around my waist so I was bound to the chair. I had flexed my hands when they tied it, hoping to get a little wiggle room so I could start working on the knot. I watched them walk away through my lowered eyelashes. I wanted to see where they were putting my gun.

"In case you don't already know who I am, you can call me, 'Your worst fucking nightmare.'"

He bared his small teeth as he smiled and my mouth went dry. He was crazy. I knew that on a rational level simply by his politics, but now I knew it on a visceral level that made my skin crawl. The bodyguard with my gun held his assault rifle in one hand and my gun in the other. He was walking back to stand by King when his phone buzzed. He set my gun down on top of a filing cabinet and took out his phone. He glanced at it quickly and then stuck it back into his pocket. Then he put both hands back on his assault rifle and looked my way.

"My problem at this moment is that you broke into my property," King said. "You're a trespasser. As far as I'm concerned I have the legal right to shoot you dead for breaking and entering and drawing a gun on me."

"For a guy who is stashing dead bodies, I'd have thought it would be a lot harder to break in here. You might want to bolster your security." I slipped one finger through the knot and started working it. I feigned nonchalance hoping he wouldn't notice how furiously I was trying to free myself.

"Obviously, I didn't suspect some greasy Italian peasant girl could figure it out. You surprise me."

"You have no idea." I mumbled it, but on the inside I was stunned.

Not so much at the ethnic slur, but at the fact that he seemed to know who I was.

He read my mind. And he knew it. He gave another malevolent smile.

"Yes. Gia Valentina Santella. I know very well who you are. I also know that you still think your homeless friend was killed by Mafioso. And that you are so wracked with guilt that you visit her grave twice a month. Let me relieve you of that guilt. One of my men killed her."

Rage spread throughout my insides making me feel as if I would burst. My blood pounded in my ears. If I weren't tied to this chair, I would've smashed his teeth out with my forehead.

The final battle's time and place must remain a deep secret until the last possible moment if one is to be victorious.

At my name, I saw Sasha's head jerk upright. She might not have recognized my face, but she knew my name. I saw her back up against the wall.

The three men saw where I was looking.

"Sasha, your grandmother's friend here is going to help you tell us where your laptop is. Because if you don't, she will die. Since you don't seem to care about your own death, maybe you care about hers."

"She doesn't care. We barely know each other."

The blurry whir of his hand came at the same time the back of his palm struck my mouth. This time I tasted blood and my teeth reverberated from the blow. But I noticed when I lifted my head again that my hands had a bit more mobility. The knot was loosening.

I met his eyes. They gleamed with excitement. I realized then he got off on violence. And knew I was in big trouble.

27

BANG

THE ELEVATOR DINGED AND TO MY RELIEF, KING WAS DISTRACTED. HE must not have been expecting anyone.

When the doors slid open I stifled my gasp.

Mayor Evans. He drew back when he saw me. My cheek throbbed. Blood dripped down my nose onto my lap. My eye was nearly swollen shut. I'm sure it wasn't pretty. The mayor's gray hair looked greasy, he had dark circles under his eyes, and his shirt had a stain on it. Things apparently hadn't been going well for him the past few days, either.

"Why is she here?"

"Not your concern," King waved his hand at me.

"It is my concern."

"Not anymore. You made it my concern." King busied himself wiping some of my blood off his knuckles.

The mayor looked dismayed. I noticed he refused to look over at Sasha.

"This has got to stop," the mayor said, wincing.

"I told you to stay away. Let me handle this. You'll get what you want."

"You need to let her go." The mayor finally glanced over at Sasha.

"I'm getting pressured. The editor at the campus newspaper called me to ask about her. He called *me*. He knows something."

Go Baumann! I didn't care what anyone said—the press still had power. And these two men knew it. And were afraid. While they were distracted I got another finger in and was now very close to loosening the knot binding my wrists behind my back. The effort was making me strain and make faces so I was relieved at the distraction and that nobody was paying any attention to me.

"I'll let her go as soon as she tells me where her laptop is and who else knows about her story."

"She didn't tell anyone," I said. "Not even her editor. If her editor knew, he would have held it over you to get her back. Trust me." Both men turned to me. I stopped fiddling with the knot so they wouldn't suspect I was nearly free.

"That makes it a lot easier," King nodded at the two men with guns who shifted forward. "You just spent your last poker chip. We have no use for either one of you anymore."

The men had raised their guns and I spoke in a rush. I sounded plugged up from my bloody —and possibly—broken nose. "But I found her story. I found her laptop."

Sasha shot me a startled glance. I hoped she would go with it.

King held up a palm and both men lowered their guns.

"It is a damn good story," I said. "It pretty much lays out everything you both have done. It contains campaign finance reports and the names of the people in those barrels on the other floor. I emailed it this morning to every media outlet in the Bay Area. Along with a note that I was heading over here to get Sasha." I glanced at the clock on the wall. "Most of them should be getting into the office right about now and reading their emails."

"You're bluffing." King's voice sounded confident, but there was something in his eyes that betrayed him. Maybe he was worried.

"Am I?" I raised an eyebrow. "As I said, the story lays out in great detail how the mayor is under your control. How your shell companies have profited the mayor's coffers: his personal finances, along with his campaign finances. In return, the mayor has agreed to be at your beck and call when he is re-elected. To be your puppet, so to speak.

"Isn't that right, Sasha?"

She nodded with wide eyes.

I paused. King narrowed his eyes at me.

"But the real meat of her story. The thing that's going to win her the Pulitzer is that she found out that in your efforts to help the mayor get re-elected, your crew of turdwads decided to clean-up the city. Except your idea of cleaning is a whole hell of a lot different than most of the world. You're starting with the homeless people of color and probably moving on from there."

The mayor was green. "I didn't know any of this."

"Bullshit." The word was so quiet I almost didn't hear it. It was the first time Sasha had spoken.

"At first, I didn't know. And when I found out I told him to stop. But he won't." The mayor glared at King, one of his bushy gray eyebrows lowered. "I never agreed to this ..." he sputtered. "To murder."

King gave a slight shrug. "We're just giving you want you wanted. You wanted results. You didn't dictate how we would go about getting those results."

"This is unacceptable. That's why I came here." The mayor shot me a glance to see if I was buying it, I bet. "To put a stop to this."

Two could play that game.

"If that's true, then tell Mr. King to let Sasha and me go." I was so close to untying the knot. I tried not to look at my gun on top of the filing cabinet. If I broke free and darted for it, I might be able to beat King to it.

Evans frowned. "I can't. If what you say is true, and the media has the story, I'm done for. I can't pretend to go on like normal. They're on to me." He wrung his hands. He turned to King. "You need to get me out of here. Out of town. Out of the country. You owe me that at least."

King pressed his lips together and narrowed his eyes. "I don't owe you anything. I've paid in full."

My efforts to wiggle free of the knot hit a snag. Something was still too tight.

"You have to help me," the mayor said to King. "I need to leave town immediately. I have all my money tied up in an offshore account. I can access it in a week, but I need to leave town now before they arrest me. I will make it worth your while." He put his head in his hands. "I wish this would all go away."

He turned to me. "It's your fault. If you hadn't sent the story to the media, we could let you go. We could go on." He shot a glance at King.

I narrowed my eyes. "Do you mean that? That we could walk out of here like nothing? Me and Sasha?"

Boy, this guy was dumb. He would let us go if we promised to not tell on him? He nodded. Barely.

"I was bluffing," I said.

The mayor shot a glance at me. "What?"

"You heard me. I made all that up about sending it to the papers and letting people know I was coming over here. I only said it so you'd keep us alive. Now you can let us go. I promise not to say anything. I bet Sasha agrees that it's worth our lives to keep that story buried forever."

She stared at me for a second, but then said, "Yes, of course."

King shook his head. "This is absurd. Of course, they are going to say something. How can you be so stupid, Evans?"

My question exactly.

The mayor turned to me with a confused look on his face.

"I was bluffing. Honest," I said.

King was moving toward me and I didn't like the look in his eyes. I had to sound more convincing. "But, it's not going to be that easy. Sasha is trying to make it as a journalist. You have to promise to feed her scoops every once in a while. To keep her in the loop so she gets the dirt before anyone else. And, you need to stop killing people."

"Yes, yes, of course." The mayor was so eager for an escape plan out of the shit storm he was in, that he would believe anything I said. It was too rich.

King was at my side then. "Enough of this nonsense. She's playing you, you ignorant fool. You are possibly the stupidest man I've ever met." He shot a glance at the mayor and then turned back to me, rubbing his finger on my cheek and then grabbing my mouth so hard it hurt.

With his back to the mayor, he continued to speak to him, but his eyes raked over me. "You have no say in it, anymore. You lost that. You will do as we say." He punctuated his words by drawing back and slapping me. I glowered and he smiled. "And you will sit back and shut up while we do what we need to do."

The blast of the gun, two quick shots, was deafening.

28

HOT BREATH

My first thought was Sasha, but when King turned, I could see the two gunmen on the floor with bullets in their foreheads. The mayor stood above them, legs spread, arm extended with my gun in his shaking hands. His hair mussed so it stood up on one side.

"You won't be telling me what to do anymore," The mayor said. He pointed the gun at King.

At the same moment, I finally loosened the ropes enough to wiggle free.

With King focused on the gun pointing at his forehead, he didn't notice me. I was up in one fluid motion and charged him. I had my hands up in fists and my leg swung around and up and caught him in the side, in the kidney, right when he turned toward me.

It didn't seem to budge him. I spun around as he grabbed for me and his fingers closed around air. Instantly I regretted attacking him. I should have let the mayor keep him at gunpoint. But there was something about the way King was inching closer to the mayor that pretty much convinced me the mayor's control of the gun was short-lived.

I lunged for King again, and tried to flip him over me as I'd practiced a million times with Kato. But this time, I got a punch to the neck that sent me spinning back and re-evaluating my plan. Keeping my hands in front of me and staying on the balls of my feet, I kept my eyes glued on his hands and feet, trying to predict his next move.

He charged, coming in faster than any man his size should be able to move. I ducked and spun, tucking myself under his arm and using his own force to tug his shoulder down. He stumbled and I dropped limp and out of his grip. Then immediately I stood up straight and yanked his head down. He bent at the waist and I pummeled the back of his neck about four times and then jerked my knee against his face.

I heard something crack and saw blood drip onto the floor. Without waiting for him to stand up, I darted toward the mayor. On my way, I leaned down and scooped up one of the semi-automatics. When I got to the mayor, who was standing there wide mouthed, I yanked the gun out of his hand.

He stared at me with relief until I poked the gun into his nose. "Don't even breathe." Behind him I saw King creeping closer.

"Back up, King. I happen to know this Barrett M82 is capable of sending rounds right through the mayor's fat head and into yours like slicing butter."

I drew back slowly.

"Both of you, over in the corner." I didn't take my eyes off them, but in my peripheral vision I searched for a way to keep them secured. There was nothing. The guns were all I had. Just as I thought that, King lunged forward and I shot him in the leg with my hand-gun. The boom of the gun was deafening in the small space. He crumpled to the ground. "Next one is right between the eyes." I gestured with the semi-automatic. "With this big boy."

I gestured to the wall. "Scoot back to where you were. Now."

I needed to free Sasha and get the hell out of there. I spoke to her without taking my eyes off King and the mayor, who were now backed up against the red brick wall.

"Sasha, if I toss you the key will you be able to unlock your ankle?"

"Yes."

I fished it out of my back pocket and backed toward her as far as I could without putting the row of filing cabinets between me and the two men. King was grimacing, holding his leg and glaring at me. He scooted back and then stood, using the wall to help him stand.

I leaned back and tossed the key toward Sasha.

"Did I come close?"

"No."

Damn.

I heard her give a huff, straining. "Wait. I think I can get it."

I waited.

"Got it."

"Let me know when you are done." King stared at me, making me nervous. I'd just shot him and he was looking at me like he had the upper hand. It worried me.

I heard metal against metal. "I'm out." Her voice trembled with excitement.

"Go to the elevator and press the down button. We're getting out of here."

The elevator dinged behind me.

"Get in and punch the button for the first floor."

"Okay." Her voice was trembling.

I backed toward the elevator, keeping my gun trained on King, who was fiddling with something behind his back.

"Hands in front of you. Now."

But he was already behind the mayor. His arm was wrapped around the mayor's neck and he pressed something that looked like a shard of glass to the mayor's jugular. A tiny red gash appeared.

"Hit the close door button now," I commanded.

"I'll kill him," King said.

That was his play?

I stepped into the elevator as the doors whooshed closed. I turned toward Sasha. "You okay?"

She looked like she was holding back tears, but she nodded.

"It's going to be okay. You're safe now." I tried to make my voice sound convincing and then just decided to change the subject. "Where is your laptop anyway?"

"In a locker at the BART station. My source told me I was in danger. He said I shouldn't go into San Francisco at all. That they were after me. That I was being followed so I ditched them long enough to hide it."

I gave her an admiring glance. "Damn, you're good."

She beamed, but then grew somber. "He warned me and I think he paid with his life."

"Why do you think that?"

"That's why they took me from the protest instead of having me meet them later. They said they'd been suspicious of him and saw his texts to me. I think they did something to him." Tears filled her eyes.

"Don't worry, we'll find him."

She looked relieved for a minute, but I thought about how there were more barrels with bodies than people missing. At least ones I knew about.

"Who's your source?"

She looked uncomfortable shifting from foot to foot and not meeting my eyes.

"Never mind," I said, waving my hand. "Baumann told me all about you guys protecting your sources and going to jail and all that stuff."

She gave a small smile. "You talked to Baumann?"

Just then the elevator stopped, the doors opening on the first floor. I moved Sasha behind me and stuck my head out into the darkness, listening. When I didn't hear anything, I gestured for Sasha to follow me. I couldn't waste time trying to find out how to open the big garage door so I'd have to make a break for the window I'd come in.

As we stepped into the garage, which felt twenty degrees cooler, I spotted the light coming from the window. I grabbed Sasha's hand and yanked her as we ran, hoping there was nothing in the dark that would trip us. But this time, with dawn breaking, I could see faintly and it looked like a clear path. When we reached the window, which was about five feet off the ground, I crouched and cupped my hands together.

"Use this for your foot and then grab ahold of my back to pull yourself up."

"Okay." She sounded scared. A sound made me freeze. I listened in the darkness, but nothing stirred. We needed to get out of there and fast.

Sasha put her foot into my cupped and interlaced palms. A tiny sob escaped her. "I can't."

"You can. I promise you. You can."

"I'm so weak." I heard a sound again and my adrenaline spiked.

"Now, Sasha. Now. I'll lift you. Go now."

For a second, she wobbled and I was worried she'd topple over, but then I felt her other foot on my back and I shot up, sending her propelling toward the window. "Grab the window sill."

"I got it." I felt her weight leave my body at the same time I felt hot breath on my neck.

"Run, Sasha! Run!"

29

SCAR FACE

I DUCKED BUT IT WAS TOO LATE. AN ARM YANKED ME BACK. I FELT something cold and sharp on my neck. I tried to ignore it as Sasha's feet pounded the pavement and then disappeared from my view. *Go, Sasha. Run like hell.*

A rough cheek pressed against mine and I caught the faint whiff of blood and something like what I imagined death would smell like.

"You will pay for my leg." The voice rumbled in my ear. I could feel his excitement pressed against me. I remembered the glimmer in his eyes upstairs when he slapped me. I'd been right. He did get off on violence.

"Where's the mayor?" I tried to sound nonchalant.

"Dead."

I somehow had already known the answer.

King drew back, keeping his arm on my neck, and walked backward, pulling me with him. He panted a little in pain. I must've really fucked up his leg. I could feel his breath on the back of my head, ruffling my hair. He obviously didn't know it wasn't in his best interest to have his face that close to my thick skull.

I wrenched my head backward, smashing it into his face at the same time I kicked behind me and landed a blow to his knee. I felt shearing pain on my face as I did so, but managed to twist free.

I darted toward the staircase, which was a faintly lighter structure in the dark. The last thing I wanted to do was stay in this nightmare building, but I needed to get away from him and the stairs were the easiest way.

I scaled the first flight and stood at the top of the stairs legs spread, hands in fists before me, eyes straining to see him in the darkness below. As soon as he hit the stairs, I'd hear him. As I learned earlier, it was impossible to be quiet on the stairs.

The screech of the garage door opening made me jump. I paused for a second, unsure what to do. Did I run? As the light poured in from outside, inch by inch as the garage door rose, I searched the vast floor below for any sign of King. When the sound of the garage door quieted, I heard the distant wail of sirens. A police car pulled into the garage space, triggering overhead lights.

The police car skidded to a halt and James flew out of the driver's side door, gun drawn.

"King's down there somewhere. He can't have escaped," I shouted.

But there was no sign of him. I leaned over searching the floor below, turning in a circle from my platform on the top of the stairs. The garage was empty. King was gone. The elevator. That's when I saw it directly under me. He must have taken the elevator and the sound had been muffled by the garage door opening.

Rushing down the stairs, I reached the elevator at the same time James did and we punched the button. It took a few seconds for the door to slide open, meaning it was no longer parked on the first floor where I had left it. King had definitely taken it somewhere.

James reached for my face but drew back before he touched me. "Jesus Christ, Gia. You're hurt. You're bleeding pretty good."

"Yeah."

I shrugged. I swiped at my cheek and my hand came back full of blood. That's when I noticed blood on the ground. I pressed the sleeve of my oversized sweatshirt up against my cheek.

The elevator opened before us. Stepping inside, I studied the options. James followed.

That's when I noticed there was a basement level. Mother fucker. I punched it before James could say a word. We sat there in awkward silence for a few seconds, me holding my shirt sleeve to my cheek, which was starting to hurt like hell.

"Thanks for coming," I said. It was the biggest understatement of the century.

"Yeah." He looked away and then back at my cheek. "I think you should go back up, get in my car, and call for an ambulance."

"I'm fine. The blood is stopping."

I wasn't sure it was, but it hadn't soaked through the thick fabric of my sweatshirt sleeve yet, so that was good.

"Next time you need my attention, why don't you text instead of email? I could've been here a lot earlier."

I shrugged. "I was in a hurry to get Sasha before the TV stations got my email with her story. I set the email on a timer so it wouldn't go out too early. That gave me time to get to her first."

"You were pretty confident."

"With the numbers and initials she had scribbled on her calendar, I knew she was meeting with King at one of the buildings the mayor owned down here. Eddy was a street not a person. 12 was an address, not a time, and KKK didn't stand for Klu Klux Klan, it stood for Kraig Kristopher King. I looked at all the other buildings the mayor owned. This was the only one that appeared abandoned and was fortified like a prison yard. Yet last night there was a whole hell of a lot of activity coming and going from here. I knew something was up."

I hadn't been bluffing about sending the emails, but at the same time I knew I had taken a huge risk and gamble.

"Got an extra gun?" I said.

He eyed me, but reached down and extracted a small pistol from an ankle holster, handing it to me as the elevator jolted to a stop. When the door whooshed open, we both flattened ourselves against the walls of the elevator. When nobody shot us, James gestured that we should move inside.

A small underground cavern lay before us, with curved stone ceilings and walls.

Stepping to one side, I kept my back to the elevator and my gun extended. James stepped to the other side. It didn't take long to see the room was empty. A door lay opposite.

A table of computers lit up the room with an eerie greenish glow from their swirling screensavers. A huge TV hung on one stone wall. A large chair was pulled in front of it. The other wall contained a map of the city. I recognized some street names but nothing else on the map made sense. It contained what looked like streets or paths with strange names that snaked throughout the city, and, as far as I knew, didn't exist. I spotted the general location of my place on Russian Hill and there were only a few red lines. Most of the red lines seemed to start in the Tenderloin and spiked out into other parts of the city.

"Tunnels," James said under his breath. And then he pointed his chin toward the door at the far end of the small stone cave. We raced to the door. I stepped aside as James nudged it open. It led to a tunnel that took off in two different directions.

"Wait here." James gave me a look.

"Whatever." I took off to the right side. The walls of the tunnel were brick, the arched ceiling concrete and the floor dirt. Red lightbulbs hung from the ceiling every ten feet or so. Sprinting, I ran with one hand holding my sleeve to my cheek and the gun in my other hand. It grew colder and soon I could see my breath as I huffed along.

I didn't hear James behind me so assumed he'd headed the other direction. I was on my own. My feet were silent hitting the packed dirt as I ran. It felt as if the air was growing warmer and the tunnel angled upward. I rounded another corner and was met by a door. An ordinary wooden door. With an ordinary handle. Leaning over holding my knees, I caught my breath, not taking my eyes off the door. A drop of blood from my cheek splattered on the dirt before me. I waited. It was only the one drop.

Holding my gun in one hand, I twisted the bronze doorknob and slowly pushed the door inward. It opened into a small dark space. The red light from the tunnel showed it was a janitor's closet with a mop, broom, bucket, and cleaning supplies. Something nagged at me, but I was too wound up to pay attention.

A slice of light on the floor and wall showed another door lay on the other side of the closet and that it was ajar. What kind of Lion, Witch and the Wardrobe shit was this? My heart thudded. King had probably come this way. I could almost feel his lingering presence.

Gingerly, I pushed the door open a few inches and listened. I didn't hear anything. I pushed with all my might at the same time I stepped in and whirled in a circle, gun drawn before me. Nobody. I was in a basement. A few bicycles were locked against a pole along one wall. Including a red bicycle. We were in the basement of the Eddy Street apartment. I rushed upstairs to the lobby.

I peered up the staircase, searching for movement. King must have fled out the front door. I bet this was why they wanted Sasha to meet there: so they could've dragged her through the tunnel to the Forgotten Island building.

Meanwhile, King had gotten away.

30

SIXTH SENSE

Before I reached the front door, I heard something that made me freeze. A creak from the stairs above. I leaned over in time to see a figure draw back from the very top of the staircase.

Along with the echo of more footsteps, a long shaft of sunlight shone down the stairwell as I heard a door slam. I raced up the stairs and didn't stop until they ended at a door to the roof.

A combination lock hung open on the door latch.

I shoved open the door to the roof and ducked, expecting gunfire. When nothing happened, I crouched and peered out the one-foot gap at knee-level, blood racing, fear spiking through me. I didn't see anything except a rooftop heating structure.

The warrior must be alert for those who wish to deceive him. The enemy is always searching for an opportunity to deceive so one must never underestimate the cunning of one's enemy by making light of his power and strength. A warrior must have a clear head to accurately see the enemy.

Stepping through the gap, I pressed my back against the cold concrete wall that jutted up onto the roof from the stairwell. Holding the gun before me, I strained to listen, hoping for some sound that would indicate where King was. The structure containing the stairwell was in the middle of the roof so that meant he had to be on the other side. Keeping my back on the concrete, I inched toward the left side, gun up by my face.

A creepy feeling, some sixth sense made me step away from the wall and look up at the same time King hurtled his body down at me. He'd been perched on top of the structure that housed the stairwell.

We both landed with a thud on the rooftop. The impact knocked the wind out of me and sent my gun spinning across the roof. Out of my reach.

As I struggled to get away, King flipped me over, straddled me, and stuck his gun in my mouth.

"Fun and games are over now."

A cold fear swept across my insides. The metallic taste of the gun filling my mouth made me gag. He released the safety and I closed my eyes. I wouldn't give him the satisfaction of seeing my terror.

I braced myself.

The whirring sound didn't make sense at first and then my eyes popped open.

Danny's drone.

It hovered only a few feet above us, it's red light flashing. Recording.

The gun was pulled from my mouth and fired, the sound momentarily deafening me, the echo obliterating any other sound. I saw King's lips move but heard nothing. The drone darted and dipped. Then, the weight on me was gone and King was standing above me, firing at the drone again.

His legs straddled me, but he was distracted, staring at the drone, waiting for it to swoop closer.

In one fluid motion, I bent my left leg at the knee, wrapping it around so my calf rested on his thigh and my foot was on his hip. At the same time, I kicked my other leg toward his crotch, arching my foot so it rested against his buttocks. Meanwhile, I reached for his ankle and yanked at the same time I pitched my hips forward, knocking him off balance. A classic Budo move executed perfectly. His back thudded onto the rooftop as I rolled to a stand.

In an instant, I dropped and was on him, my leg wrapped around him so that I was pinching his neck between them. Try to get away now, dickhead.

The gun he'd dropped was only about three feet away but I couldn't reach it without moving off of him and letting him go. My legs were wobbling already. I wasn't sure how long I could hold him before my strength gave out.

The whirring above me reminded me of Danny and his drone. But then the drone swooped away as an army of police rushed through the rooftop door in SWAT gear with gigantic guns aimed at me.

"Hands up!"

I thrust my hands up into the air. Then James stepped out of the door, saying something. The officers circled King and yanked me away. They had him cuffed in seconds.

I sat, shaking, in a corner.

James was suddenly at my side.

"You, okay?"

I nodded.

"The paramedics are on their way."

I frowned.

"Your cheek?"

"Oh."

"I think you're going to need stitches. I also think you've lost a lot of blood."

"Oh."

Two paramedics headed my way. I didn't fight or argue. I had nothing left.

31

TETANUS

Perched on the edge of the hospital bed, I gingerly touched my cheek and the fat bandage on it. I wished there was a mirror. Despite the doctor's refusal to answer me, I was pretty sure I was going to have a hideous scar. I could tell by the sympathetic look the nurse gave me when I asked. When I said I'd no idea what King had cut me with, they hooked me up to an IV, as well. Later, James told me they'd found a rusty piece of metal with blood on it in the garage.

Fanfuckingtastic. A scar and tetanus.

Yawning, I suddenly felt like I hadn't slept for a week instead of only a night. I decided to lie down and curl up in a ball until the nurse came back. I'd asked her to check when I could be released. I'd drifted off when a commotion outside my door woke me.

"Nuh-huh, you are not going to make me wait. You can't tell me I'm not family. Why would you say that? You think I'm not family because I'm black and my daughter's white?"

Darling.

The nurse said something I couldn't hear and then Darling said in a lower voice, "Listen, I'm the closest thing that girl has got to family and I'm going in there whether you like it or not."

I smiled.

She pushed through the door and had me wrapped in a big squishy hug before I could even say hi. I came up for air and no, I wasn't crying. Must have been my allergies acting up.

Darling pulled back and looked at me. "Mmmm hmmm. You gonna have a big ass, scar, baby girl."

I shrugged. "How's Sasha?"

Darling swiped at her eyes. "She gonna be alright. They're keeping her overnight for observation. She's got an IV and stuff like you. They say she's dehydrated and they are giving her antibiotics because of her pinky toe. It's a little infected. But I think she's going to be alright."

I breathed a sigh of relief. But I had a confession to make.

"Darling, I knew about her toe. They ..." I looked past her and scrunched my face up, bracing myself. "They sent me her toe yesterday. I'm so sorry. I was afraid to tell you."

Darling drew back, eyes wide. "They sent you my grandbaby's toe?"

"Yes." My voice was barely above a whisper. She had every right to lay into me.

"Oh Lord, have mercy. Honey, I'm so sorry."

"No, you don't understand," I stammered. "It's all my fault. You don't get it. It's my fault. Because I went to James. They told me it was because I went to the police. They were following me."

I spilled the whole thing and looked down at the hospital floor, waiting for Darling to answer. After exhaling loudly, she grabbed my hand between her two hands and patted it. "It was all meant to be. Whatever you did, it worked. You got my grandbaby back. And you both still alive. That's all that matters."

I looked up. That's when I noticed Bobby standing in the doorway. Darling must have seen the look on my face because she turned. "Oh, good. You're here now."

She headed toward the door. "I'm going to let you two chat." She turned back to me. "Sasha is in room 320. She wants to see you when you're up to it."

"Thanks, Darling." I had a hard time taking my eyes off Bobby.

As soon as Darling left, he stepped inside shutting the door behind him.

The look on his face told me the ball was in my court.

"Darling called you?"

He nodded.

"I'm glad." I said, figuring honesty was my best play.

He smiled. "I was thinking the same thing."

I patted the bed beside me and he came over and sat down, not taking his eyes off my face. He looked at my cheek. "You okay?"

"I think so."

"Good."

Taking a deep breath, I spoke. "I was thinking about something while the doctor was stitching me up. It hurt like hell. Way worse than when it happened. Maybe all the adrenaline was gone or something but it really hurt and I was dumb enough to say I didn't need it numbed."

"Oops."

"Yeah. Not the only thing I've been dumb about." I glanced over at him under my eyelashes, but he didn't react. "When the pain was at its worst, I was wishing you were here holding my hand, telling me that everything was going to be okay. But then I realized I'd blown it with you."

Again, he didn't move a muscle.

"As they were fixing my face, I thought about what my major malfunction was and I realized that I'm afraid."

"Well, no kidding. I could've told you that. Hell, you already said that."

I raised an eyebrow and went on. "True. But here's why I'm afraid—in case it counts: Everyone I care about dies, Bobby. You know that. You've seen it. So, I realized that this irrational dumb part of me is afraid you'll die, too."

There. I said it.

He swallowed. 'You're afraid to make a commitment to me because of that."

"It's dumb, I know." I reached for his hand. "I'm sorry."

"You said everyone you care about dies. Do you have to make a commitment to me to care about me?"

"No!" I'd said it too loudly.

Then I thought about what he'd said. Of course, I cared about him whether I had a commitment to him or not. I couldn't help it.

He leaned over and kissed my forehead. I drew back and cringed a little.

"I'm sorry," he said. "Does your whole face hurt?"

I didn't answer.

"Well, good thing there are a lot more places I can put my mouth besides your face."

Gingerly he touched the bandage. "You're going to look bad ass with a scar."

I laughed despite myself, but then grew serious. "So, you're cool with having a girlfriend who looks like Tony Montana?"

"All I have in this world is my balls and my word and I don't break 'em for no one," he said, quoting my favorite line in Scarface.

"Very funny," I said. "Your accent sucks by the way."

Instead of answering, he leaned over me and kissed my neck, his mouth trailing down to my collarbone, and soon we were so caught up in each other's bodies, I didn't realize someone had opened the door until I heard the nurse gasp.

32

IN THE WIND

"KING'S GONE."

It was James.

"What?" I had been half asleep when my cell rang. "I thought he was in jail?"

"Something is going on. Somebody with a lot of power pulled some strings and he made bail this morning."

I sat up shaking my head trying to clear it. Bobby sat up beside me, yawning.

"Who grants bail at ..." I looked at my clock. "Before eight in the morning?"

"Judge Conner apparently."

"So, he's gotta be on King's payroll."

"For sure. Proving it will be another matter. The San Francisco District Attorney has already put the judge on probation. Judge won't be in court again soon, maybe ever."

"When is King supposed to appear again?"

"Next week, but he's in the wind."

James explained. Since he'd made bail, all King's bank accounts had been cleared out and his four houses—in Berkeley, Washington,

D.C., New York City, and Miami—had mysteriously sold overnight after his arrest.

The FBI had put him on their most wanted list. The CIA was searching every corner of the world. Even Interpol was looking for him.

He was wanted for twelve murders. The ten homeless and poor that he'd murdered and put in barrels, along with the mayor's murder and the slaying of Sasha's source, a man pretending to go along with King in order to stop him. His name had been Josh. Guy was a goddamn hero if you asked me.

After I hung up, I sat there thinking about what James had said until Bobby pulled me over to him and woke me up properly.

———

SASHA'S STORY ran top of the fold, in the main San Francisco paper, and then was picked up by every paper in the world, it seemed. The first TV station to have it, however, was Channel 5. I'd called Jimmy the photographer and told him all the details so he came out with the full, detailed story at noon the day the paper had it. The other news stations had tried to hobble something together by their five o'clock news, but ended up quoting Sasha's story in the San Francisco paper that first day.

King's group had fractured into ineffectual subsets that tried to rally in protest of his arrest, holding signs that said, "We are the power. You cannot stop us."

Antifa put out a reward for information on King's whereabouts. The information didn't say "Dead or Alive," but that's pretty much what they meant. They were pissed beyond belief that King's goons pretended to be Antifa.

Within a week, the protests by the few follower's King still had—at least those who admitted it publicly—only drew a few dozen people. Counter protesters apparently decided that even showing up was giving the small hate group credence and attention they didn't deserve, so they stayed home

As details of King's ethnic cleansing operation spread, people stopped defending him at all. The protests died out completely within two weeks.

But Sasha's story of corruption prompted investigations throughout the country, sending any other hate groups underground.

Baumann was interviewed on CNN, the BBC, and the Today Show, about his young star reporter because Sasha refused to go on the air and she begged Baumann to step in for her. She didn't want the attention. And didn't want people to know what she looked like. She worried fame would hurt her chances of investigative pieces when she graduated in two years and accepted the position waiting for her in the Paris bureau of the Associated Press.

Every time there was a show about Sasha and her story, I bought champagne and cheese and crackers and huddled in the back room of the salon with Darling to watch. Sasha refused to join us. After one 60 Minutes episode featuring Sasha's investigation, I stood and paced Darling's small back room. I balled my hands into fists. I wanted to punch something.

"Baby girl, you brought her home. She stopped that King. It's all good. What on earth are you all bothered about. You look like you want to punch somebody in the nose."

"I didn't bring her home soon enough."

"You hush now."

I'd turned the pinky toe over to the police, but it would haunt me forever.

"My Sasha is one tough cookie," Darling said, her chest puffing out in pride. "She doesn't even want to go to counseling any more. She wants to find King and make him pay."

"I bet," I said, shrugging on my leather jacket and striding toward the door. "I'll see you tomorrow night, right?"

"With bells on."

"Who is your date Miss Darling?" I knew many men were in love with her, but she hardly gave any of them the time of day.

"Surprise."

"Must be the governor, then."

"Ha!" She snorted.

"Sasha coming?"

"She's on deadline."

"See you tomorrow then." I stumbled a little pulling on the door.

Darling gave me a look. "You okay to get home?"

"Yeah." For once, I was stone cold sober. Plus, it was a short walk home. My place had finally been finished. I'd moved in last weekend. Before my things were even packed, I'd sold my Russian Hill apartment to the neighbor next door. He said he was going to bust down the walls and double the size of his place. More power to him.

"You give my dog a big fat smooch from his mama, you hear?"

"Fine."

Django had moved back in with me when I got my new place. He seemed to have forgiven me or else he was a really good actor, wiggling all over the place and putting his paws up on my shoulders to kiss my face when I came home.

Walking out into the crisp, cool night air, I pulled up the collar of my jacket and tucked my fingers inside my sleeves. Fall was in the air. Halloween was in a few weeks. The night sky glowed orange above me. In the distance, the tall buildings of the financial district were dotted with lights in the windows. Overachieving accountants burning the midnight oil or janitors busy cleaning.

Here in the Tenderloin, the buildings were dark. With only an occasional night owl, like Danny, still awake. Most of the homeless had tucked into their ratty blankets and cardboard boxes or curled up in a pew in St. Boniface church.

The streets were mine.

As I got closer to my building, I could see the hulking darkness of the building in the Forgotten Island. The creep factor of the building had not diminished for me.

Even though the police had finally removed the barrels of bodies, faded yellow police tape was still strung across the fence and garage door. The whole place still loomed dark and forbidding—a place where death had been welcome.

Shortly after Sasha had been found, I'd happened to drive by the building on my way to check on the construction progress at my new place. I'd involuntarily shivered as the building's bulk cast a shadow over my car.

Later that day, I'd gone to the city to search the property tax records. I wanted to know who had owned it before the mayor. For some reason, the most recent property tax files were missing. The next most recent file dated back to 1956. A man named Donald Jamison had sold the building to a group called SF Industries. About as generic sounding as you could get.

Before that, a lumber company had built the building after the San Francisco fire.

What had been there before was lost to the ages.

A small part of me wanted to buy the building, tear it down and construct something new. But I also knew that some evil cannot be removed. Some places just exude darkness and are best avoided.

33

ILLICIT SEX

I TWIRLED IN FRONT OF THE MIRRORED WALL IN THE PENTHOUSE LOBBY. The Armani suit fit like a dream. Even so, I didn't want to completely give in, so I didn't wear a shirt or bra underneath it. From the front, it was completely modest. Everything that should not be seen in public was covered.

However —if I turned a certain way—well, it would give those old codgers on the board something to think about at night.

And I'd had the pants hemmed so my favorite Jimmy Choo stilettos peeked out at the bottom. To finish off the look, I wore earrings that were shimmery silver strings that flowed like a waterfall to my shoulder pads.

When Dante stepped out of the elevator I puckered my fire engine red lips at him. "So?"

He smiled. "Looking good, G."

Gingerly he touched the jagged line running from my cheekbone into my hairline.

"This is sexy."

"Ha." I rolled my eyes at him.

The raised slash on my cheek ached a little and felt odd when I smiled, but for the most part I'd forgotten about it.

I winked and looped my arm through his. "Let's go crack some fucking heads."

After the door into the boardroom closed with a heavy whoosh behind me, I stood with my legs spread and my arms across my chest. "Gentlemen."

There was an uncomfortable murmuring around the table.

"My associate Dante Marino has been hard at work since our last board meeting and has uncovered some interesting findings I'd like to share with you."

The men shifted uncomfortably. I smiled, flashing my white teeth at each one of them in turn.

Then I pouted. "Wait? You don't seem happy about this?"

I walked over to the large floor-to-ceiling window, looking out at the Golden Gate bridge, keeping my back to them. "You couldn't possibly be worried about what he found, could you?"

I whirled back around.

"You see, the so-called research involved taking a look, a deep, penetrating look into your expense accounts. Wow, was it fascinating. It sounds like you all have been having an absolute ball since my father's death. Trips to Bali. A fleet of new cars for each of you. A vacation home in Steamboat Springs. Even the rental of the penthouse at the Top of the Mark here in the city, for well, geez, Dante, what was it? A year straight?"

Dante nodded, his eyes deadly calm.

"Yeah. That was a doozy. I'm sure there was lots of illicit sex in that room. Your poor wives. It was probably the most egregious use of the money my modest and upstanding father earned working sixty hours a week until the day he died." I scrunched up my face. "Especially since our private investigator found that Mr. Henley liked to use the penthouse to host underage parties where he drugged young women, stripped them and photographed them for his private collection. So, Mr. Henley, why don't you get your saggy old ass out of here before I call the police and hand over the video footage we have of you."

A blue-haired man with a bad comb over and a red face looked as if he might choke, but managed to push back his chair and rush out of the room past me.

"Now, which one of you is Tad Carrillo?"

A man in his sixties with neatly trimmed short hair and Elvis Costello glasses stood. "Ma'am?"

I could see his Adam's apple bob.

"And who is Ed Alford?"

"Here." A man with a deep, husky voice answered and stood. His mane of gray flecked hair swept back from his face above his stylish glasses.

"And one more," I said, smiling. "Who is Shawn Long?"

A man with brushed back brown hair stood. "I'm Shawn."

I clapped my hands together. "Wonderful!"

"You three are the only board members who didn't screw this company over. You are all welcome to stay and help me turn this place around." I smiled at them. Tad Carrillo's shoulders sagged in relief. Then my smiled faded.

"The rest of you get the fuck out of my boardroom before I call the police and have each and every one of you arrested."

Startled looks were exchanged. Eyes wide. People froze.

"Now!" I screamed. They scuttled like cockroaches out the door.

Once the door closed I let out a big sigh. Dante walked around and handed the three men envelopes.

"Please open your envelopes."

I watched gleefully as they each extracted the check inside. The stunned looks were sweet.

"Gentlemen, thank you for your loyalty to this company and to my father's memory. I've given each one of you a token of my appreciation."

"Excuse me?" I turned. It was Ed Alford. "This is really unnecessary. Extremely generous, but unnecessary. I know you want what's best for the company and this is possibly not the wisest use of the funds we are working with. Especially in light of some of the misappropriation you've uncovered."

"That's sweet of you to say, Mr. Alford, but that isn't from the company. That's from my own account."

The three men exchanged looks.

"And don't worry. You'll earn that. I'm going to rely on you and turn to you heavily in the next few months so we can salvage what's left of this company. I'll be here working along beside you every minute for the next six months, but then I'm hoping to turn it over to you three. You'll be in charge of finding new board members and so on.

Don't worry. I'll make sure you still have a life, too. I'm not going to take you away from your families. My father always said family first and that is a value we need to make sure we keep. But when you are here, I expect the best of you, agreed?"

The men murmured agreement.

I gestured at the chairs. "Let's get down to business."

34

SWANSON PLACE

It took two attempts for Bobby and I to get out the door to the grand opening party. I blame it on the dress.

When Bobby ran one finger down my hips and discovered I had nothing on underneath, it was impossible to resist his kisses.

As I stepped onto the sidewalk in front of Swanson Place, the black velvet slithered across my thighs and felt delicious against my skin. Going commando had definitely been the way to go. The dress itself was pretty modest, down to my ankles and a modest neckline, but it plunged to my lower spine in the back. I wasn't a nun.

I was eager to see the twelve residents. I'd sent them to the Esalen Hot Springs in Big Sur where they'd soaked in the hot springs, and had massages, facials, manicures, pedicures and a chance to relax. On the drive back, I'd had their drivers stop at Sak's Fifth Avenue in Carmel where personal shoppers had helped them pick out modest wardrobes.

So far, all twelve of them had gone through two weeks of training for their jobs at the businesses on the street level. There was nothing requiring them to work at Swanson Place, but most had been eager to apply for the jobs offered. They'd interviewed the same as everybody else for jobs in the hair salon, the market, the flower shop, the rooftop garden, and the restaurant.

The newspaper had already dubbed the restaurant, named Lorenzo's after my father, the latest hottest sensation. After failing to convince Dante to move to San Francisco, I'd lured a chef away from Chez Panisse in Berkeley and told her to go to town, creating the restaurant of her dreams. Her creation was a luminous, blue-lit underwater-feeling, sensation. In the two weeks, the restaurant had been open, I'd already made back my investment.

When I stepped inside, Kato rushed over and tried to hand me a glass of champagne. I ignored it and kissed him on both cheeks.

"Where's Suzie?" I asked.

"Over there," he said. I'd hired his wife, Suzie to manage the restaurant. She was with Dante. He'd agreed to help oversee the first month of the restaurant's opening. They were talking to a crew of wait staff and looking like a rock star in her sleek silver dress. She saw me watching and winked.

I'd hired Danny to be the DJ and he was in the corner spinning music that I'd never even heard of, but knew was just right.

"How's it going?" Bobby stepped up to Kato and the two shook hands. As they caught up on sports news or whatever dudes talk about, I scanned the restaurant, looking for the twelve residents. As I picked them out of the crowd, one by one, I smiled.

Everything was in place.

Tonight, after the celebration at the restaurant, the twelve would go spend the first night in their new apartments. I had fresh flower bouquets and fruit and chocolate waiting for them in their new homes. Each resident had signed a lease for a year. It would be up to them whether to renew the lease. I didn't want them to feel trapped. I only wanted them to have a leg up. I'd handpicked all twelve and knew that this opportunity was what they needed to turn their lives around.

Swanson Place had turned into a pilot program. Cities across the country were carefully monitoring the success of our project. It was starting out small, with only twelve residents, but it would be possible with future projects to go bigger, and house even more people.

The board, now back up to seven members, had agreed that if the development was a success—financially, but also in helping homeless get off the streets permanently—that we would replicate the project, constructing similar developments in other parts of San Francisco and eventually in other cities.

The other cities who had expressed interest—Los Angeles, Phoenix, Atlanta, New York, Chicago, Minneapolis, Miami—had also talked about partnering with us so that some of the costs could be offset with municipal funds. The developments were something I was excited about. But they were also a way for me to honor Ethel.

And maybe if enough people were helped during my lifetime, I could let go of some of the guilt I felt about all the homeless murders.

Because even though her body hadn't been in one of those barrels, if what King had said was true, Ethel had been the first one they'd gone after. She was the experiment before they refined their technique. If I'd taken time to properly investigate her death, maybe, just maybe I'd have been able to stop the rest of the murders.

I gave Bobby a kiss and told him I'd be right back. I headed for the restaurant's bar, which was surrounded by four nearly room-sized aquariums containing exotic fish. I saw a few of the building's residents: Ron and Serena and Joey and Matt. They were talking to City Council member Julie Kragen who had taken over the mayor's duties until the next election. Off in a dark corner I saw something that made me pause. Darling and George, with a white bandage on his head, looked pretty cozy together. She leaned in as he brought his lips close to her ear and he had his arm on her lower back. Who knew?

I never did find the blond woman who saw the men kidnap Sasha, but when George had been released from the hospital, James had showed him mug shots of a few of King's cronies and he'd been able to identify two of them. Better than nothing.

A waiter with a tray of champagne passed by and I plucked a

glass off with a wink. Then I raised the glass, high above my head. "Ethel, this is for you."

I took a sip and standing in the doorway of the restaurant, closed my eyes until I was sure the urge to bawl had passed.

Then I felt Bobby's hand on my back.

"Gia, you did something good here." He jutted his chin at the room.

Watching the smiling faces shining under the sparkling lights, the mingling of people from different stratospheres of the city, I could almost feel the hope permeating the room. It was only one small corner of the world.

But it was a start.

The story continues in *Vengeance*, the next Gia Santella Thriller. Head to the next page for a sneak peek or order today by clicking the link or scanning the QR code below!
www.amazon.com//B0767MXG14

Stay up to date with Kristi Belcamino's new releases by clicking the link or scanning the QR code below!

https://liquidmind.media/kristi-belcamino-newsletter-signup-1-first-vengeance/

(You'll receive a **free** copy of *First Vengeance: A Gia Santella Prequel!*)

Did you enjoy *Vigilante*? Click the link or scan the QR code below to let us know your thoughts!

www.amazon.com/review/create-review

VENGEANCE CHAPTER ONE

I was in my happy place.

La Bella Rossini in North Beach. The best Italian food in San Francisco.

The first bourbon had warmed my insides and flushed my cheeks. My second glass of liquid gold sat sparkling in the candle light. A man I was crazy about was smiling at me like I was the best birthday present he'd ever received. The food was obscenely delicious.

Bobby reached his fork over the table to spear the massive scallop bathing in butter on my plate. I swatted him away. "Back off if you want to keep that hand."

Hiding my smile, I took him in. Sometimes when he showed up at my door, I thought that there was no way such a beautiful man was all mine. He looked like a young Johnny Depp except he had longish auburn hair.

"What?" he said, tilting his head.

"Nothing." No need to tell him what I was thinking or he might get a big head.

I chiseled off the tiniest piece from the hockey puck-sized scallop. I closed my eyes, and let out a small groan as it melted on my tongue.

When I opened my eyes, Bobby was smiling and shaking his head.

"Don't do that in public. Please."

"I have no idea what you're talking about." It was the truth.

"If you want to stay long enough for dessert, you're going to have to stop doing that."

"Doing what?"

"Moaning as you eat. Every dude in this restaurant is watching."

"Oops."

I looked around. The restaurant around us bustled with people celebrating this glorious late fall weather. The wall-sized windows were open, extending the dining room onto the bustling North Beach sidewalk. Diners sat at the sidewalk café tables. Although I didn't live in this part of town anymore, it was very much my home. My people.

A small group of chicly dressed diners at a table near us spoke Italian. Although many of the North Beach old timers still spoke Italian, I didn't hear it very often. This group was definitely from the *bel paese*. They had *la bella figura* down pat. From the women's glossy hair and designer clothing to the men's polished, custom-made shoes. Italians.

They stood out since most San Franciscans who came to eat in the Italian section of town donned the city's unofficial laid back utilitarian uniform: skinny jeans, environmentally friendly slip on canvas shoes, flannel shirts, and fitted down jackets.

I was somewhere in between in my nicest leather pants and high-heeled boots. It was my dress-up uniform. We were celebrating Bobby's birthday, so I'd ditched my motorcycle boots and faded jeans just for him.

I took another bite of my scallop and tried not to moan this time after I noticed that Bobby might be right: A few men at nearby tables watching me under hooded eyelids.

"Gia!"

A slight moan had slipped out. "I'm trying!"

"I can't help it if I enjoy my food." I gestured at my plate with my fork. "I mean it's practically orgasmic."

"Exactly." Bobby said, making an exasperated face.

Over our dessert of pistachio-dotted cannoli, I pushed an envelope toward Bobby.

"Happy birthday." My cheeks grew hot. For some reason, I was both embarrassed and nervous for him to open it.

He slid one finger into the envelope and withdrew a thick stack of papers, reading the top sheet. I knew the first piece of paper listed our airline reservations to Italy.

"You bought me a ticket." He gave me a look. He'd thought I was going solo. "When I said I couldn't afford it, I didn't mean you should buy my ticket." He looked a little pained, instead of happy. Damn it.

"Shut up, it's your birthday. Dante's my best friend and I want you to be my date for his wedding so my treat. It's actually more of a birthday present for me."

He rolled his eyes, but he seemed less distressed. He glanced down at the paper again. "We're leaving tomorrow?"

"Surprise!"

"I don't even have the time off work."

"I already talked to your boss. He was totally down for it."

Bobby raised an eyebrow.

"It's cool," I said. "He was really nice about it. In fact, he suggested a side trip we should take to some small island of the coast that has a marine research lab specializing in something. Like studying planktoskeletans or something. It's not far from where we are staying in Positano. A train ride, maybe." I'd forgotten exactly what it was, but I'd scheduled the trip as part of our itinerary. Bobby worked for a marine biology research lab studying how to prevent the depletion of oxygen-producing plants in the ocean. "The oceans are the lungs of planet earth," he once told me.

"You mean phytoplankton?"

"Yeah, I think that was it."

"Cool." His eyes were wide and glassy with excitement. "Did you know the Mediterranean is arguably the most diverse sea basin when it comes to species and culture? I bet that lab has some research we could use in our studies. If we could figure out a way to keep the oceans clean, we can make up for—or at least counteract—some of the ozone depletion over Antarctica. The ocean provides half of all the oxygen on earth but we are destroying it. Carbon dioxide and industrialization are demolishing the ocean's ability to provide us the oxygen we need."

I tried to look interested. "Wow." I gestured toward the stack of papers. "There's more."

He turned to the next page. It was a printout with color photos. He sat back, his mouth open as if he were about to say something.

"It's where we're staying." I said, maybe a little big smugly.

"You're joking, right?"

I couldn't stop grinning. "No joke."

He shook his head. "It's a freaking castle."

"It's actually a villa."

"It's incredible." He flipped through the papers. "Is there a picture of our room?"

"Bobby, the entire place is ours."

"You're shitting me."

"Not shitting."

"For three weeks?"

"Yep. Happy birthday."

He put the papers down. "It's too much."

"It's not. Really. You should see Dante and Matt's place. Freaking Taj Mahal of the Amalfi Coast."

He pressed his lips together. I reached over and rubbed my fingertips over his creased brow. "Say thank you. Please."

Bobby leaned back again, let out a big breath, and then, finally, smiled. "Thank you."

I relaxed back into my seat, as well. The smile that always made me melt, also made everything perfect in my world again. My heart was full to bursting. If I could purr, I would. I'd have to make do with ripping his clothes off and having my way with him. Not a bad compromise, I thought, grinning to myself. I snaked my foot under the table and rubbed it against his leg.

"Should we blow this joint? I can think of something I'd rather be doing right now." I gave him my sexiest smile.

"Check please." He raised his arm.

We were curled around each other as we walked through the restaurant. As we stepped outside onto the sidewalk, I impulsively turned to kiss Bobby. I went up on tiptoe. His silky hair brushed against my cheek. At the same time my lips grazed his, a horrific screeching noise and ear-splitting blare of a horn was accompanied by Bobby jerking me off my feet and flinging me away.

I slammed against a wall, stunned by the impact, and blinded by headlights and then crushed by Bobby's weight on my torso. I instinctively put up my arm to shield us. The air was filled with blood-curdling screams and the shuddering crunch of crumpling metal. The headlights stopped a few feet away from my face and the wall I was against shook.

Distantly I registered the headlights came from a gray SUV, wedged cater-cornered into the wall supporting the restaurant's alcove doorway where we had taken cover. Or rather, where Bobby had tossed us. The passenger side door was inches away from Bobby's leg. A few feet closer and we'd have been underneath the engine. A few feet the other way and the SUV would have careened through the open French doors and taken out the entire crowd of diners inside.

The screaming, coming from God knows where, grew louder and shriller.

I pushed my way out from under Bobby, frantic for air, hyperventilating with panic.

Bobby grabbed my arm before I could scramble to my feet. "Are you hurt?" He took my chin in his hands and looked into my eyes.

I couldn't speak. Only shook my head. I tried to stand but my legs were Jello. I collapsed back onto the sidewalk.

"You sure you're okay?" His voice was shaking. I didn't answer, too staggered by what lay a few feet away. Limbs stuck out helter-skelter from beneath the vehicle, along with the mangled frame of a café table. The front window of the SUV had disintegrated, jagged glass shards along its edges. I couldn't see anybody inside.

"Good God." Bobby sprung up and was at the bumper. Several other men joined him. They lifted the car and set it off to one side. A man miraculously scrambled out from under the SUV. He had a tire mark on his chest. He took a few steps and collapsed. Another man lay unmoving. Bobby leaned over and checked the man's pulse and then shook his head. A woman in a torn dress, stood screaming, pulling her hair and staring at the dead man. A small crowd gathered. The dead man's eyes were open and seemed to stare straight at me. I looked away. That's when I saw her.

With everyone concentrating on the victims under the vehicle, nobody had noticed her. She lay on her back on the sidewalk near the building, staring at me, her lips moving. Her clothes bloody. Her legs splayed at an unnatural angle. As I met her brilliant green eyes, she reached out her arm toward me. She gave me a look I knew I would never forget to my dying day: a combination of desperation, determination, and wide-eyed horror.

I crawled over to her on my hands and knees. She was speaking Italian, talking so quickly I couldn't hear her over the still blaring horn or make out the words in the foggy, surreal haze that surrounded me. I lifted her head a few inches onto my lap and gently smoothed her hair off her forehead, trying to soothe her as I looked around for someone who could help her. Everybody was busy with the man who had crawled out from under the car. Finally, someone disabled the vehicle's horn and whomever had been screaming finally stopped.

I heard the faint sounds of sirens in the distance. In the back of my mind I remembered something about not moving an injured person, but it was instinctive to lift her head out of the pool of blood on the sidewalk and smooth her hair back in an attempt to calm her. Her eyes were so green they seemed to glow.

She continued to speak in Italian, sounding angry, but her words seemed like they were coming from far away. I brushed a bloody clump of hair out of her face.

As I did, I felt something sticky. That's when I saw that the other side of her head, the one near the wall, was laid open bare. A huge chunk of her scalp and brain were gone. I swallowed my revulsion, looking down on her, her features upside down, her green eyes were wide and glossy. As she rapidly spoke to me in Italian, her words finally came together for me.

"*Sei tu.*" It is you.

I'd never seen her before in my life, but I nodded and continued to brush her hair back on the side that was still intact. "It's okay. It's okay." I tried to keep my voice reassuring even though it wasn't okay. Not at all. Part of her brain was missing. She was babbling. All I could do was comfort her.

"*Sei tu.*" It is you.

Her green eyes grew wide and she looked angry. She struggled to sit up, but I held her down by placing my forearm across her upper chest. The movement had caused something to ooze out the side of her head. I didn't know what it was, but I knew it wasn't good. Moving was the last thing she should be doing.

"Shhh," I said, searching my memory for remnants of what Italian I remembered. "*A chi bene crede, Dio provvede.*" It was something my own mother had whispered to me as a child when I was upset. I didn't know what it meant exactly, but it was all I had. A small part of me wanted to slip out from under her and run away from her as fast as I could. My body pleaded with my mind, begging me to get up and run as far away from this horror-movie scene as possible.

But my heart ordered me to sit tight. My Budo beliefs gave me resolve, fighting against my body's natural repulsion.

Determined to comfort her, I held her as gently as a mother holds her own newborn. My job was to comfort her. I repeated my hopefully soothing words: "*A chi bene crede, Dio provvede.*"

But instead of calming her, my words seemed to infuriate her. She said something angry, spitting a little, glaring at me. "*Sei tu.*" It is you.

Then her body went limp. She'd been straining against me to lift her head, her neck muscles flexed, but now she relaxed in my arms. In the distance, the sirens seemed to draw closer.

Hurry. Hurry.

A nasty taste filled my mouth. I tried not to look, or think about, the side of her head. Instead, I concentrated on her face. Her brilliant green eyes, lined thickly with black eyeliner. Her perfectly shaped eyebrows and lips with red lipstick, forming an "O."

The cacophony of sirens was close now. On the street, only a few yards away now. But looking into the woman's eyes I knew it was too late. She stared at me intently, her gaze full of both fear and fury. I cradled her head as the light left her eyes and the life seeped out of her.

Bobby came over and tried to move me, but I shook his arm away and continued to stroke the woman's hair on the one side. I sat there on the cold sidewalk until the paramedics came and gently lifted the woman out of my arms.

VENGEANCE CHAPTER TWO

I stepped out of the shower, shivering, trying not to look at the mound of clothing on my bathroom floor, but still getting a glimpse of my shirt, soaked in blood and something else. I closed my eyes and swallowed. I didn't want to think about what else might be on my shirt after it served as a pillow, cradling that Italian woman's shattered head on my lap.

"Gia?" Bobby's voice was faint on the other side of the bathroom door. I'd locked it. Probably for the first time ever.

"I'll be out in a second." My own voice was wobbly. I slipped on my old fuzzy robe and stepped around my clothes to unlock the door and push it open. I stood there, hair dripping wet, and stared at Bobby waiting on the other side of the threshold.

"Can you ...?" My hand waved weakly at the pile of clothes on the floor.

He nodded, eyes wide, his Adam's apple bobbing.

I stepped toward him, stumbling a little. He grabbed my arm, steering me toward my bed. Soon I was tucked in under a warm mound of blankets pulled up to my chin, my head propped on a massive stack of pillows.

Bobby whistled and Django hopped up on the bed wiggling and kissing my face.

"Down, boy." Django settled in beside me, warming me instantly. I was still shivering.

"I'll join you in a minute," Bobby said. He handed me a travel mug with a shaking hand. "Meanwhile, drink this."

I lifted my head and he stuck a straw in my mouth. He'd made a hot toddy. I eagerly sucked the liquid down, anxious to blot out the images of the dead woman that kept surfacing. He watched me drink it, forehead furrowed.

"Aren't you fucked up from all that?" I asked.

He shrugged. "It was pretty bad, but I sort of saw some of that as a paramedic."

For the first two years of college, he'd thought he wanted to be an EMT and had worked one summer as a paramedic.

I lifted the empty mug toward him. "Can I have more?"

He nodded and headed toward the kitchen area of the loft. He set the mug down on the counter and pulled a plastic trash bag out from under the sink. I tried not to look, but out of the corner of my eye I saw him in the open bathroom door lifting my clothes up with one hand and dropping them in the trash bag. He crossed the wide-open main space of my loft, opened the front door, and tossed the trash bag into the hall. Then he was at the stove in my kitchen, fixing me another drink.

After I sucked that one down, he stripped. Only a few hours ago, I'd hoped for this moment, my sexy man naked in front of me. Now, I couldn't even manage a smile at the sight. He pulled on flannel pajama bottoms and a soft T-shirt and crawled into bed on the other side of me. I was firmly sandwiched between my dog and my man, both pressed up against me. It was possibly the safest place in my world, but I felt like I was a balloon bobbing wildly in a fierce storm, drifting, unreachable, unmoored.

Bobby reached over and with the press of a button on my phone clicked off the loft's overhead lights. A small glow-in-the-dark Milky

Way was on the ceiling above my bed came to life. I stared at it, willing it to soothe me like it usually did.

Instead, all I could see was the Italian woman. Her face looming before me in the dark.

Bobby sensed my unease. "You okay?" His words filtered across the dark expanse of my bed, drifting, reaching into my foggy head.

I didn't answer.

"You sure you don't want to have the hospital check you out?" His voice sounded worried. I'd fought like a wild cat when they tried to stuff me into an ambulance outside the restaurant until finally Bobby had rescued me.

"That woman ..." I finally managed to say.

"You did everything you could," he said. "You gave her a small measure of comfort during her last moments."

"She was the driver, right?"

"That's what it looks like."

A sob escaped me. "How many people died?"

"The guy with the tire mark on him? A miracle. The EMT's said he was damn lucky. He'll live. Somehow missed his vital organs. He's a swimmer and has crazy strong chest muscles or something."

"How many, Bobby?"

He sighed. "I think two. Her and the guy under the car."

"Oh, my God," I said.

"Listen, Gia. I know this was a horrible, horrible night."

"Her head ..."

"You did everything you could."

I sat up on my elbow, peering over at his dark form. "Why are you so calm?" My words were tinged with anger. He was there, too. Even having worked as a paramedic, how could he be so cavalier about it all?

"Don't take this the wrong way," he said. "But I'm feeling pretty damn grateful. A few seconds, a few inches, it could have been us."

That sobered me.

"People die, Gia," he continued. "Unfortunately, you know this better than most people. You've had to deal with more death than anyone I know."

I bit my lip, my anger fading.

"I mean give yourself a break. You are learning how to live with that. It was only a few months ago you were afraid to commit to me because you thought it meant I would die, right? But here I am."

I nodded, but felt uncertain.

"And tomorrow we're heading to Italy to celebrate Dante and Matt's wedding. That's a big step for you."

He was right. Was it only a few months ago I was so afraid that I'd dreaded going away with him for a weekend? Now, we were spending three weeks together.

"I couldn't save her ... her head. It was gone." I laid back down, staring at the glowing planets on my ceiling.

"Listen," he said, leaning over and pulling the covers up to my chin. "I know you're going to try to save everyone you can because that's who you are. You have the biggest heart out of anyone I've ever met. But here's the hard thing that you have yet to face: You can't save everyone, Gia."

I hated to admit it. But he was right. It had been proven over and over in my life. If I had any say in it all, a whole hell of a lot of other people I loved would still be walking this planet.

He leaned over and kissed my forehead and then lay back, reaching under the covers for my hand and holding it tight. His words and his touch soothed me. With Bobby around, I truly believed I could love and have a normal life.

But as he fell asleep and began to snore softly, that certainty fled. Even though I still held his hand, I felt utterly alone. No matter how hard people over the ages had tried, we all died alone.

Even though I held a stranger as she died in my arms and tried to comfort her in her last moments, she died utterly alone. It was bitter and inevitable and there was no escape. No money. No love. No good fortune could prevent it. Nobody was exempt.

I stared up at the stars glowing on the ceiling and the utter enormity of this realization flattened me. At the same time, I couldn't shake the feeling that the woman's death was a bad omen. Bobby was right: people died. People I loved died. They died unjustly. Unfairly. Nonsensically. But he was also wrong. I didn't have to face it or accept it. And I never would.

———

The sun was rising to the west, casting an orange pink glow over everything for as far as I could see. The skyscrapers in the financial district to the west reflected the ethereal light. My rooftop haven, filled with pots of flowers, was bathed in the sunrise colors and yet it felt like a dark cloud hovered right above my building. Sitting under the lanai that extended from the greenhouse, I eyed the potted fern where I kept my pack of cigarettes hidden in the foliage, but resisted.

Usually this was my hideaway, my safe spot, one of the few places I found soothing, but this morning I couldn't get the dead woman's green eyes out of my head.

Bobby was still asleep downstairs, his silky auburn head barely poking out from the covers. I'd grabbed a fuzzy blanket and taken Django up the stairs. In a few hours, we were leaving for Italy.

Sitting alone in the cold, I gave myself a pep talk. I vowed to not let last night's events ruin our trip. This vacation was supposed to be a fresh start for me. When I bought the tickets, I'd realized that for the first time since my parents died, that I'd felt free. Free to live my life. Free to let my guilt go. I'd stopped all my bad habits. I drank like a normal person (a glass or two of wine with dinner each night.) I allowed myself one cigarette a month. I was in a healthy relationship with a man I was crazy about. I was finally, after so long, getting my shit together. I wanted to celebrate this new chapter in my life by treating my boyfriend and myself to a spectacular trip to Italy.

He was the one who had shown me it was okay to care about someone.

For so long, I was worried that falling for Bobby was his death sentence. He'd proven otherwise. And I *had* fallen for him. Hard. In a way I never had before.

He'd been telling me he loved me for about a month. The first time he did, I stared, stunned and speechless. He'd laughed. "Don't feel like you need to say it until you feel it. Or feel comfortable. I'm cool with that. I just can't keep my feelings in any longer and I had to let you know."

It wasn't until this past week that I realized I loved him back. And had for a long time. It was the first time I'd loved a man. It made me giddy and filled with energy. I wanted to let him know so badly. But every time I tried to say the words, they failed me.

Along with having copious amounts of amazing sex, scarfing down the most delicious food on the planet, drinking the finest wines, and celebrating my best friend's wedding, my goal on this trip was to finally say those three words out loud to Bobby.

Downstairs later, standing in my doorway, my neighbor Thanh-Thanh was hugging Django like he was a person. He was up on two legs and had his paws on her shoulder.

"Oh, brother," I said. "He's going to be intolerable when we get back."

Thanh-Thanh giggled. "Django is a very courteous dog. Always genteel. He is super."

I raised an eyebrow. Eight months ago, when I met her, she hadn't even spoken a lick of English and now she was putting me to shame with her vocabulary.

"Your English is brilliant."

She beamed. "I'm studying very hard."

"I can tell," I hitched my duffle bag on my shoulder. Bobby was waiting below, but I was reluctant to leave for some reason. "You know where everything is. The phone number for the vet is on the fridge. If you need a break, Darling's number is up there, as well. As a matter of fact, you might consider bringing him by the salon if you're getting your hair done."

My close friend, Darling, owned a hair salon and was obsessed with my dog. Maybe even more than Thanh-Thanh. Leaning over, I scratched Django behind his ears and tried not to feel sad. It was just a dumb dog. Not even a person. An animal!

Thanh-Thanh gently pushed me toward the door. "Leave. I have it under my management. Completely. Everything is adequate. I will take excellent care of him. I guarantee."

I cast one last glance at my apartment and my dog. Everything would be fine. If anybody could be trusted with my dog it was Thanh-Thanh. She was the reason he was alive. She'd rescued him a few months ago when the first building we lived in burned to the ground.

Still, I couldn't help feeling a frisson of foreboding as I watched her close the door on me. Maybe it was the woman dying in my arms. Maybe it was nervousness about this trip with Bobby. Whatever it was, there was definitely something there, hovering in the shadows, beating its black wings. But I didn't know if the dark shadow that had just crossed over my grave meant something bad was headed her way. Or mine.

Are you loving *Vengeance*? Scan the code below to order your copy today!

ALSO BY KRISTI BELCAMINO

Enjoying Kristi Belcamino? Scan the code below to see her Amazon Author page!

Gia Santella Crime Thriller Series

Vendetta

Vigilante

Vengeance

Black Widow

Day of the Dead

Border Line

Night Fall

Stone Cold

Cold as Death

Cold Blooded

Dark Shadows

Dark Vengeance

Dark Justice

Deadly Justice

Deadly Lies

Additional books in series:

Taste of Vengeance

Lone Raven

Vigilante Crime Series

Blood & Roses

Blood & Fire

Blood & Bone

Blood & Tears

Queen of Spades Thrillers

Queen of Spades

The One-Eyed Jack

The Suicide King

The Ace of Clubs

The Joker

The Wild Card

High Stakes

Poker Face

Standalone Novels

Coming For You

Sanctuary City

The Girl in the River

Buried Secrets

Dead Wrong (Young Adult Mystery)

ALSO BY WITHOUT WARRANT

More Thriller Series from Without Warrant Authors

Dana Gray Mysteries by C.J. Cross

Girl Left Behind

Girl on the Hill

Girl in the Grave

The Kenzie Gilmore Series by Biba Pearce

Afterburn

Dead Heat

Heatwave

Burnout

Deep Heat

Fever Pitch

Storm Surge (Coming Soon)

Willow Grace FBI Thrillers by Anya Mora

Shadow of Grace

Condition of Grace (Coming Soon)

Gia Santella Crime Thriller Series

by Kristi Belcamino

Vendetta

Vigilante

Vengeance

Black Widow

Day of the Dead

Border Line

Night Fall

Stone Cold

Cold as Death

Cold Blooded

Dark Shadows

Dark Vengeance

Dark Justice

Deadly Justice

Deadly Lies

Vigilante Crime Series by Kristi Belcamino

Blood & Roses

Blood & Fire

Blood & Bone

Blood & Tears

Queen of Spades Thrillers by Kristi Belcamino

Queen of Spades

The One-Eyed Jack

The Suicide King

The Ace of Clubs

The Joker

The Wild Card

High Stakes

Poker Face

AUTHOR'S NOTE

In the beginning of this book is a fictional obituary for a fictional character: Ethel Swanson. In 1999, a newspaper, The Central City Extra, was founded to report on the Tenderloin's improvement efforts. Some years later, at the request of Rev. Glenda Hope, a long-time mover and shaker in the neighborhood, the paper began including obituaries.

"The obits were a way to put a face on the neighborhood that is populated by ordinary, low-income folks who never got their name in the newspaper while alive and the respectful farewell our obits provided were welcomed by the family and friends left behind," said Geoff Link, Executive Director of the San Francisco Study Center.

Many of the obituaries were published in Death in the Tenderloin: A slice of life from the heart of San Francisco.

In the book's foreword, Link writes, "This book celebrates the Tenderloin at its most tender. It was inspired by the obituaries published in the Central City Extra—monthly newspaper for the neighborhood's fixed-income and no-income population. This is a hardscrabble script.

"The Tenderloin is San Francisco's poorest neighborhood, a high-density, human services ghetto where hundreds of nonprofit and public providers serve a citywide caseload of homeless people in addition to treating the tribulations of the area's 30,000 residents.

"Our hood is a mere few dozen square blocks cemented between downtown and Civic Center. Nob Hill is above. Skid Row below. Death in the Tenderloin is our eulogy this historic, notorious neighbor and its medley of people, absolutely the most diverse community San Francisco, the heart of the city in more ways than one. We want you to come away with a sense of how difficult life is out here on the edge."

To put a face to "fixed-income" and "no-income" residents of the Tenderloin who are memorialized in this book, Link and the Study Center Press has agreed to allow me to publish a few excerpts from the book. I include them here in the hopes that you will consider donating to the Study Center.

You can also support the center by buying the book, Death in the Tenderloin.

————

Obituary excerpts from "Death in in the Tenderloin"

Teresa of the Tenderloin

HANK WILSON There's a job that can't wait, Hank Wilson told the volunteer from Network Ministries. Upstairs, in the Ambassador Hotel that Wilson managed, George was in bad shape, deathly sick, incontinent. He needed a bath. They went upstairs. George had gotten out of his filthy room and was crawling down the hallway naked, covered in his excrement.

They got him into the bathroom. Wilson drew the bath and with effort pulled George into the tub and started cleaning the tenant who always gave him a hard time.

"That's who Hank was at the core," Rev. Glenda Hope said. She recalled the story in her Network Ministries office, sniffling and dabbing her eyes, not long after Wilson's death. The incident was more than 20 years ago, and the volunteer was one of hers.

"That's what we saw in him. This guy who has so ripped him off —and was screaming obscenities and cursing him—and Hank was tenderly washing the shit out of his hair like a mother with a baby, and then drying him off with fluffy towels. ...

Hope paused as memories from 28 years of knowing Wilson, often working side by side with him in the Tenderloin's deepest trenches, flooded her mind. ...

"He was a giant in my life," Hope said. "More than any other person I've known, he showed me the meaning—taught me—forgiveness and unconditional love."

Henry "Hank" Wilson, gay activist, innovator and humble servant of the Tenderloin's sick, poor, and homeless, died at Davies Medical Center. A nonsmoker who had survived the ravages of AIDS, he was 61 when he died of lung cancer.

Wilson's achievements are so epic some friends have called him the Mother Teresa of the Tenderloin.

Musician who almost made it

GARY MAGUIRE narrowly missed his 15 minutes of fame as a musician. The drummer once tried out for the Jefferson Starship band and had just about everyone's vote, Stephanie Olson, his wife, said after Maguire's memorial at the Coronado Hotel where they had lived for six months.

"Grace Slick liked him and the others in the band wanted him, too—he could play all the instruments but excelled at the drums— but the execs didn't," she said. "So he didn't get it. If he had, I told him he wouldn't have lived very long, leading that kind of life."

Maguire didn't have a long life, as it was. He died at the hotel, presumably of liver complications, at age 49.

Several generations of his family were from South San Francisco, so he knew a lot of people. He worked in construction for a while, then was homeless with her for several years. Even so, they made the best of it. Once, when they had a little cash, they took bicycles to Woodside and rode around looking at fabulous houses.

The city's Homeless Outreach Team got them into the Coronado and Maguire started to change, got edgier. He was cheerful enough indoors, but not out in the hood where danger lurked. He was sensitive about cruelty and injustice.

Among her fondest memories is when they were homeless in Burlingame and bought a big, six-person tent—Olson 39, is 6 feet tall herself—and pitched it by the railroad tracks. They had nothing but each other.

"We'd lie there and talk about nothing and everything. He was so happy and generous. There was nothing he wouldn't do for me. And nobody bothered us ... We had no water or electricity," she said. "But I was so happy to be with him and wake up to the songbirds."

A troubled man

LOUIS O. GUZMAN Temperamental Louis O. Guzman likely got more respect at his memorial than he got in his 14 years living in the Turk Eddy Preservation Apartments. Cantankerous and combative, he was difficult to be around. He constantly complained and swore, and tried to hustle his fellow residents for money.

"I told him once, 'Mr. Guzman you can't go out on the street talking that way to people—you'll get beat up or killed," said manager Patsy Gardner. She said he shot back. "That's why I've got this cane!"

Guzman died at St. Francis Hospital two weeks before his 84th birthday.

Seven residents from the 20 occupied apartments in the building paid their respects at Guzman's memorial. A few recalled he had asked them for cash, others said he wanted to sell them things they didn't want, like the two old bicycles in his room.

Guzman left Hawaii 59 years ago. He has a sister there and a brother in the East Bay. It's believed Guzman worked in construction at one time. He rallied against government and disliked handouts, yet drew SSI and Social Security, totaling barely $900 monthly. Still, on a few occasions, he sent his sister $75 money orders.

"Not many saw that side of him," said Rev. Glenda Hope, who conducted the memorial.

Batman

LONDEVETTE MORGAN earned his "Batman" nickname by

keeping a vigil over the neighborhood while seated at the window of his fifth-floor Elm Hotel room.

The self-appointed street savior claimed to now many of the shopkeepers below and would tip Elm staff to any untoward activity in their vicinity.

"He saw himself as a peacekeeper," said case worker Adam Decker.

Morgan, a garrulous teller of tall tales, often would get lost in his random thoughts until someone pulled him back to his story line.

"I saw him Monday, the day before he passed," said Ricky. "He came by and gave me a dollar, sometimes it was $2. He had a good heart. You don't see many like him."

Roz, the only woman among the eight mourners, said Morgan wanted her to be his girlfriend and told her was going to marry her. But it was hard to know when Morgan was kidding or on the level, she said.

Scott Ecker, Elm services manager, recalled that once, as he was trying to catch a taxi in pouring rain, Morgan came outside and held an umbrella over him for half an hour, as a simple kindness, talking the whole time.

"His storytelling was crazy, and it was hard to know what was factual," Ecker said. "But I was fond of him."

Other mourners said Morgan had told them he had played bass in a band and had been a boxer.

A man who lived across the hall said he had had "thousands" of encounters with Morgan and "75% of them were unhappy. He could be a monster, too," he said, without elaborating. "He was very sick at the end. I think he drank himself to death."

Batman, apparently ignoring his failing health, died in bed reading his newspaper. He was 53.

Vietnam war hero with mystery legacy

ROBERT DUSSAULT. A dozen friends bid farewell to Robert Frederick Dussault, a Vietnam War hero and former Union Street antique dealer, in a memorial at the Empress Hotel where his friendliness and generosity were highly regarded.

Dussault died of "natural causes." His friends said the ravages of old war wounds reduced him in recent years, and hastened his death at 64.

They described (him) as an intelligent man with a lovely soul who volunteered to help without being asked, was courteous, invariably had a kind word for folks and would do anything for a friend. But he deeply distrusted the government and impressed people by making his conspiracy theories seem so reasonable.

(In high school), he was elected senior class president. Dussault attended UC Berkeley, married his high school sweetheart and joined the Navy, becoming a lieutenant in the SEALS. He was wounded in Vietnam and sent home for good, but he insisted on returning, and he did as "a river pilot," a move that ended his marriage... His boat was strafed, he was wounded and lost the use of his right arm.

Besides the memory of his good will ... Dussault bequeathed a mystery. He was believed to have several storage rooms full of antiques.

They called him Hollywood

GLEN BURISE had a spark. Everybody saw it. Maybe it was personality, though he wasn't boisterous, funny, or overly playful, just kind of edgy. It made you look and consider him. And that's what he wanted.

That was the image held among the eight friends and acquaintances who gathered at Civic Center Residence for his memorial. The native San Franciscan, 6 feet tall, always smartly dressed, died of lung cancer at Laguna Honda Hospital at age 56. His trademark black hat was hanging from the wall at the head of his bed. His estranged daughter had visited him the night before.

Donald Beard, who said he met Burise when he was 14, told how he got his nickname. Glen so wanted to be like his late brother, Fred, a colorful and well-known player in the heyday of the Fillmore jazz scene. But the younger brother couldn't quite pull it off, Beard said, and got called "Hollywood" for his efforts.

Burise moved into a fifth-floor unit in the 200-room residence a year ago. He was quiet and dignified and spoke like he had some education. He avoided petty fighting among the residents and brandished an occasional smirk to punctuate conversations. Over recent months, according to friends, he was in and out of the hospital, lost 40 pounds and had to wear white support stockings and blue hospital slippers down to the dining room, never complaining about his pain, deterioration or lost image.

He had another dimension, too.

"He expected you to look at him and see him, even in a crowd," said Carlita Barry. "Here, where he lived a reduced life, he continued to be himself. He didn't dissolve or disappear. And it was refreshing to see."

ABOUT THE AUTHOR

Kristi Belcamino is a USA Today bestseller, an Agatha, Anthony, Barry & Macavity finalist, and an Italian Mama who bakes a tasty biscotti.

Her books feature strong, kickass, independent women facing unspeakable evil in order to seek justice for those unable to do so themselves.

In her former life, as an award-winning crime reporter at newspapers in California, she flew over Big Sur in an FA-18 jet with the Blue Angels, raced a Dodge Viper at Laguna Seca, attended barbecues at the morgue, and conversed with serial killers.

During her decade covering crime, Belcamino wrote and reported about many high-profile cases including the Laci Peterson murder and Chandra Levy disappearance. She has appeared on *Inside Edition* and local television shows. She now writes fiction and works part-time as a reporter covering the police beat for the St. Paul *Pioneer Press*.

Her work has appeared in such prominent publications as *Salon*, the *Miami Herald, San Jose Mercury News,* and *Chicago Tribune*.

Contact Kristi Belcamino at:
    kristibelcaminowriter@gmail.com

facebook.com/kristibelcaminobooks
instagram.com/kristibelcaminobooks
tiktok.com/@kristibelcaminobooks